A Daddy for Him

The PlayPen #1

Charity Parkerson

Punk & Sissy Publications

Copyright

—Warning: This book is intended for readers over the age of 18. Some of my books contain allusions to past abuse and trauma.

Editor: BZ Hercules & Consultants

Cover art: Temptation Creations

Contents

Introduction

After recently losing his boy to another man, Rhodes spends his nights at The PlayPen, a club for the daddy/Little scene, torn between wanting what everyone else has and bitterness. Cairo has what he needs.

Rhodes is a daddy without a Little. It's a tough position for him. He's used to having that small comfort in his life. Everything else is violence and blood. As part of the country's biggest weapons dealer's security team, he's accustomed to being hard. He misses the softness of caring for someone with an innocent heart. Of course, the moment he chooses to let it go, life drops another needy Little on his lap. He's not about to say no.

Cairo has a problem only a powerful daddy can solve. It's a secret that could get Rhodes killed. But Cairo only has one shot to throw himself on Rhodes' mercy and show he can be the best boy. If he can't pull it off, then the move means he's as good as dead. He's willing to take the risk for a shot at something better. Cairo never expects how desperately he'll end up wanting to keep Rhodes or how quickly the past will catch him.

A Daddy for Him is the first book in The Playpen. This series is a spinoff from the Little Lost series, where adorable, sometimes bratty, and scared Littles meet the men of their dreams.

Author Note about Content

Warning: This story has a daddy/Little plot with mild age play that could make some people uncomfortable. There is also talk of past abuse.

Chapter One

The PlayPen looked like an exclusive country club from the outside. Inside, it was a haven for Littles. Toys and playsets littered the floor where Littles spent their time. Large round tables lined the edge of the room for daddies to play cards and drink. Rhodes had been a member for a few years. At least twice a week, he sat at the same table, playing the same card game with a group of men he barely knew. Every night, the experience highlighted his lack of having a boy. He didn't need The PlayPen to shine a spotlight on that emptiness. Rhodes went to bed with it every night since Brody left. It was okay. He was fine. Kind of. Tonight, he wasn't as sure. He felt more pathetic than ever, sitting alone and incapable of finding peace. Losing Brody sat heavily on his chest tonight. There was just something in the air. When he looked around, all he saw was his envy. A man pushed his boy on the swing. They looked perfect for each other. Their smiles were huge. Rhodes wanted to scream.

A light tap on Rhodes' shoulder pulled him from the edge. He glanced over, expecting a greeting from any of the dozens of familiar faces. Instead, he found a sweet, freckled face nearly hidden by a fuzzy brown bear's hood. The little ears on top suited the guy, and Rhodes couldn't explain that. He was adorable.

Big blue eyes met his stare. He held out a stack of cards. "Would you play Go Fish with me?"

God. His heart. The guy sounded so sweet. "I'd love to." Rhodes pushed a chair away from the table with his foot. "Have a seat. I'm Rhodes."

"I know."

Rhodes bit back a laugh. No offer to give him a name. Just "*I know*." Rhodes knew he knew. Everyone knew. As part of the Bosi security team, people kept a wide berth unless they, too, were connected to the biggest weapons dealer on the west coast. Beau Bosi employed a lot of rough and tumble guys. They were often seen around The PlayPen for various reasons.

Reason number one being, Beau was married to a Little, so they came so Kylo could play with his friends. Number two, Beau's son, Banks, owned The PlayPen. Honestly, those two reasons were pretty equal. The second one was the one that had them coming around the longest. Still, no matter what the excuse, they were well known.

His new friend dealt the cards while Rhodes studied him. Rhodes couldn't take it. "Do you have a name?"

An adorable giggle punched Rhodes right in the chest. "Everyone does, silly."

Rhodes couldn't stop smiling. "Am I allowed to know it, or is it a secret?"

"Oh." He giggled again. "Oops." He squared his shoulders and held out his hand for Rhodes to shake—like donning his big boy persona. “Cairo Kelsey. Twenty-two. Scorpio.”

The laughter beat him. He hoped Cairo didn’t think he chuckled at the guy’s expense. Cairo just lifted his mood with his adorable personality. “It’s nice to meet you, Cairo Kelsey. Twenty-two. Scorpio. Does that mean you hold grudges?” At least that was the theory about Scorpios.

“Until they turn into diamonds, and I also look amazing in black.”

He was having the best time. Rhodes picked up his cards and arranged them by number. “Who goes first?”

“Me, of course. I’m the baby.”

“Of course,” Rhodes agreed, trying to keep the humor from his voice. He missed the hell out of nights like this.

"Do you have any threes?"

"Go fish. Do you have any tens?"

Cairo chewed his bottom lip.

Rhodes swore he forgot anyone else existed. "No cheating."

Cairo's shoulders fell. He passed a ten to Rhodes. "Do you have any fives?"

Rhodes passed his two fives to Cairo.

Cairo kicked his feet in happiness as he placed the four matching fives on the table. "I'm very good at this game."

"I see that."

Blue eyes latched onto him. "What games are you good at playing?"

There was definite innuendo behind the question, but it was also mixed with innocence. Before Beau married a Little, Rhodes had never dreamed he would want this. Seeing the happiness this dynamic had brought to Beau's life and the entire household by extension had made him curious. That was how he had ended up with Brody. It was possible he wasn't very good at being a daddy since he hadn't held on to him. Interacting with Cairo made him realize exactly how badly he wanted that feeling again.

"I'm not very good at any games except for the ones played in the dark."

Cairo's guileless expression never wavered as he nodded. "We should do that next."

Damn. That had been a risk on his part. Cairo might have reacted any way. Rhodes wasn't disappointed by Cario's response. It was not like he would say no. “If that’s what you want.” He wouldn’t let Cairo walk into things blind, though. “Since you know who I am, I assume you know who I work for. Our home has a lot of armed protection. I don’t want you to be scared.”

Cairo’s serious look never wavered. “You’re very big. I’m sure you can keep me safe.”

Rhodes didn’t know whether to laugh or to growl in possessiveness. “Damn right.” No one would be touching his boy. Rhodes blinked at how dark and dominating his thoughts had turned, and how quickly it happened. Maybe he shouldn’t mess with this after all. Cairo looked so sweet and pure. Someone like Rhodes could only sully him.

“Do you have any threes, or can we go now?”

Considering Rhodes had already said he didn’t have any threes, it seemed the boss had spoken. It was time to go. Maybe Cairo wasn’t so angelic after all.

He drove a Hellcat. Cairo wasn’t surprised at all. Rhodes just looked like a guy who would drive a badass car. He was tall and all sleek muscles. Even if Cairo hadn’t already known Rhodes worked for one of the most dangerous men in the U.S., he would have guessed he worked security of some sort. He had that look about him. Eyes always moving, watching for threats. Those eyes were terrifying.

They were an indescribable mixture of blue and light gray. It felt like the guy stared into his soul each time he focused on Cairo. Cairo was in danger, and he loved it.

When they reached what could only be described as a compound, butterflies stirred in Cairo's stomach. Rhodes hadn't been exaggerating. Heavily armed guards were posted everywhere. There were so many huge buildings that each looked like mansions. He couldn't tell what was a house, garage, or what they were. He wished he felt out of his element. Unfortunately, this situation felt very familiar, but Cairo needed a strong and deadly man to protect him from another one. He had watched Rhodes for a while. The guy had a neediness in his eyes that spoke to Cairo. Cairo had been forced to bide his time. Now that his plan had been set in motion, he was scared shitless. This could go wrong in a million different ways. All he could do was his best. He could be a good boy.

Rhodes pulled into a garage attached to one of the many buildings. The door slipped closed behind them, shutting them inside. After killing the engine, Rhodes unbuckled Cairo's seatbelt for him. Cairo twisted the straps of his backpack in his nervousness. Anything could happen to him now. There was no going back. But everything had already happened to him over the years. He had to take this chance for something good. Rhodes jumped from the car and circled it to Cairo's door. He helped Cairo out, taking away some of the fear starting to grow. Rhodes looked so dangerous and yet touched him so gently. It messed with Cairo's head a little.

"Time to get ready for bed, little one. Do you have everything you need in that bag to stay the night?"

Cairo nodded. For the life of him, he couldn't get his voice to work. He hoped Rhodes didn't feel the way he shook. Cairo was so nervous, he didn't even look around on their way inside. He kept his eyes glued on Rhodes' back as they climbed a set of stairs. It didn't help there were guards everywhere, making him feel scrutinized every step of the way. He hated that feeling of being judged as he was led away to do exactly what they thought he was about to do.

Finally, they were shut inside a bedroom that looked more like a fancy hotel room.

It had a kitchen and a couch, along with a massive bed.

Rhodes took his bag from him. "Come on. A bubble bath before bed will help you sleep."

Cairo put his mind on lockdown. It was too late to overthink. Plus, he couldn't say he didn't want Rhodes. Damn, he was sexy and smelled delicious. Cairo had never had someone so beautiful care for him. He hoped he didn't embarrass himself.

Cairo stood in the center of a large bathroom. It looked nice. There was an entire wet room with an enormous tub. He wondered if Rhodes planned to join him. Cairo watched Rhodes start the bath water before returning to his side. He set Cairo's bag on the counter. Then his intense focus locked on Cairo. It became a little harder to breathe. Rhodes wasted no time. He pushed Cairo's hood off. A smile snapped to his lips at the sight of Cairo's strawberry-blond hair. No doubt it stood on end. Cairo couldn't look away from Rhodes' perfectly angled face. He should be on the cover of magazines with his dark hair shaved short on the sides but curly on top. Just the right amount of facial hair and dark skin tone that always made Cairo wonder at his ethnicity. He had to know.

"Is it okay if I ask where your parents were born? That sounds awful. You just have an amazing skin tone that has me curious. You're very pretty."

A smile exploded across his face. Straight white teeth. Wow. It must be nice to be so perfect, unlike Cairo's multitude of freckles... and scars. He hoped Rhodes still wanted him once he was unclothed. "I don't think I've ever been called pretty." He slid the zipper down on Cairo's one-piece pajamas. "Sorry to disappoint you, but I have no idea. I was raised in an orphanage until I ran away at sixteen. Beau found me and offered me a job."

"He sounds kind."

Rhodes froze with Cairo's pajamas pushed halfway down his arms. He held Cairo's stare. "He isn't. No one here is, other than maybe Beau's husband. It's best not to get that idea in your head. There isn't a single person on property who hasn't killed someone at some point in their lives. They'll do it again in a heartbeat to keep Beau safe. Do you understand?"

"Yes." Unfortunately, he did. Death and pain were all too familiar to him. "I don't take back my compliment, though."

Rhodes shook his head. A small smile lingered on his lips as he undressed Cairo. With a blank mind, Cairo let it happen. He used the only commodity he had to win Rhodes—his body. Cairo was too familiar with that too.

The moment Rhodes had Cairo nude, he led him to the tub that was already nearly full with bubbles almost overflowing. The water had shut itself off, screaming money. Cairo climbed in and sat—thankful for the heat that enveloped him. The tub was self-regulating too, damn. He loved a bath that stayed hot. He was especially glad to have the bubbles hiding him once Rhodes whipped his shirt up and over his head. Cairo's mouth went dry. The desire to run his hands all over Rhodes' torso was nearly crippling. Rhodes grabbed a rubber duck and toy tugboat that sat on a shelf inside the wet room. He tossed them in the water with Cairo before going down on his knees beside the tub. Rhodes snagged a clean washcloth from a nearby basket and went to work. He used a yummy strawberry-smelling bodywash and shampoo to clean Cairo while Cairo played. It was oddly satisfying to sink the boat. He also realized if he squeezed the duck, it would fill with water he could squirt. Letting go and reclaiming childhood was the only peace he got. It was a disassociation even money couldn't buy.

Unfortunately, one dark thought creeped in, and a million more followed. Cairo kept his gaze locked on the toys. "Why do you have toys? Do you bring boys home to play a lot?" Why had he asked that? Of course he did. All daddies were like that. Boys weren't special.

"No." Rhodes sounded sad. That brought Cairo's gaze his way. Rhodes watched his hands as he cleaned Cairo. "I used to have a boy. He fell in love with someone else: a guard for a drug lord we know. I guess he got sick of living with someone as needy as I am. I don't know. He just said I was too much and left."

An unreasonable amount of rage roared to life in Cairo's chest. It bled into his voice. "No. He was weak. You didn't deserve that."

Rhodes' mouth lifted in one corner in a sardonic smile. "Maybe I did. You don't really know me. I could be a monster."

"Were you faithful?"

"Yes."

Rhodes' response surprised him for the earnestness in his tone. It was obvious he had been hurt. He believed Rhodes when he said he hadn't strayed. Cairo doubted many men could say that. All he had ever known was monsters. He could be honest too. "Then you're better than anyone I've ever known."

Rhodes held his stare. "You're worth more than that." Rhodes let the water out of the tub and grabbed a nearby towel. It was obvious he had no idea how hard that claim hit Cairo. Maybe if a single person in his life had ever made him feel like he deserved anything at all, then life would have turned out differently for him. Maybe he would have been brave enough to escape sooner. Unfortunately, no one thought less of Cairo than Cairo.

Cairo dutifully stood when Rhodes helped him up and out of the tub. He stayed like a statue while Rhodes dried his skin. Cairo didn't break from his thoughts until Rhodes wrapped him in the towel and then used the two halves to slowly tow Cairo forward. His heart did a little flip as his gaze met Rhodes' stare. Rhodes lowered his head, and Cairo's body immediately responded. He wanted to be kissed. Cairo missed the sensation of lips against his skin. Rhodes had nice lips. Cairo wanted to touch them. Then Rhodes' mouth touched his forehead, and Cairo didn't know if he would survive the disappointment.

Rhodes hated to admit how Cairo terrified him a little. He looked so innocent and sweet. Cairo asked all the right questions and said all the things needed to win Rhodes. But Rhodes had been used and lied to before. He didn't know if this was an act. Rhodes had gone into this night expecting to soothe something inside himself. Now he wanted to save this beautiful man, and it kind of pissed him off. He hated this weakness. Caring for other people always ended up destroying him. Rhodes hadn't truly had anyone his entire life who wanted him and only him, and wanting things to be otherwise only led to heartache. Yet he couldn't stop.

"Time to brush your teeth."

He didn't miss the disappointment that flashed across Cairo's features, but he still let Rhodes lead him to the sink. Cairo dug through his backpack and found his toothbrush. The move kind of hit Rhodes. Why was Cairo walking around with an overnight bag? Did he go home with anyone who asked? Was he homeless? He looked too well cared for to live on the streets. Rhodes would know. He had survived that life for nearly a year before Beau rescued him. Some people might not consider the possibility of having to kill someone to protect their boss as being saved. If they didn't, that only proved they had never been hungry enough to know that level of desperation. Beau had his loyalty for life. Maybe Cairo understood the feeling.

Rhodes readied his toothbrush. "Why are you carrying around an overnight bag?" He kept the question casual and his gaze locked on his task.

Cairo froze halfway through brushing his teeth. He focused on Rhodes' reflection in the mirror. A hint of fear crossed his features. He spit in the sink. His shoulders squared and Rhodes knew he was about to hear a truth he wouldn't like. Still, Cairo looked as if he couldn't meet his stare. "I—" He froze and visibly swallowed. His gaze slid away.

Rhodes brushed his teeth and waited him out. He wouldn't scare Cairo any more than he obviously already had.

Cairo's gaze snapped back to his in the mirror—like he had made his decision and would stand by it. "I recently left an abusive relationship. Banks has been letting me hide at The PlayPen, but essentially, I'm temporarily homeless."

Rhodes wasn't surprised. While Cairo had a gorgeous body, Rhodes noticed a few things about him while bathing him. Scars he had seen before. Marks that looked way too familiar. He rinsed his mouth and spit. Rhodes knew how he reacted now would set the tone for whatever happened between them. He put his toothbrush away.

"You have no reason to be ashamed." Rhodes swept Cairo from the floor and headed for the bedroom. "Bedtime. You look exhausted."

Cairo didn't complain when Rhodes tucked his nude body beneath the sheets.

His bright blue stare followed Rhodes' every move as he stripped.

"Are you mad at me?"

The question hit as Rhodes turned out the light. His shoulders fell. He had tried to set Cairo at ease by moving slowly. It was obvious all he had done was make the guy's anxiety skyrocket. He climbed beneath the covers, snagged Cairo around the waist, and tucked him into his hold.

"Why would I be angry with you?"

He felt Cairo shrug. "I don't know. Maybe you might think I'm using you or something. Or maybe I'm a disappointment. I don't know. It feels like you're angry."

Fuck. Rhodes hated whoever had hurt Cairo. He kissed Cairo's temple. "I'm not mad at you." He had to add that last bit because he was fucking furious someone hurt Cairo. Rhodes slid his hand down Cairo's soft body. "I'm definitely not disappointed. You just need rest more than you need me pawing at you. I can wait to play until you're ready. Your health is more important to me than anything."

Silence met his claim. It dragged on for a minute before Cairo broke it. When he spoke, he sounded small. "You don't even know me. Maybe I'm a horrible person."

A smile snapped to Rhodes' lips. "Are you a horrible person?"

Cairo didn't answer right away, as if he really thought about it. That alone proved he was better than most. "I'd like to think I try to be good." He snuggled closer and kissed Rhodes' chest.

Rhodes lost the battle against the erection he had been fighting. "What would a good daddy do right now?" Rhodes really hoped Cairo knew the answer because he only knew what he wanted. It didn't involve patience of any kind.

Cairo's lips skimmed Rhodes' chest again. "He'd let his baby soothe himself."

Holy shit. He wouldn't make it. Rhodes didn't know what soothing him entailed, but Cairo's tone had all the ideas going through his head. "You should do that."

He felt Cairo's lips shape into a smile against his chest. He had nothing to go by, but that smile still felt evil. Rhodes swallowed. He had a bad feeling Cairo knew exactly how to wrap Rhodes around his finger.

Cairo gently pushed, urging Rhodes onto his back. "I want my pacifier." He slithered down the bed and sucked the tip of Rhodes' cock into his mouth.

A low moan escaped Rhodes before he could stop it.

Cairo didn't try taking him deeper. He simply sucked Rhodes' head exactly like a pacifier.

Rhodes was pretty sure he would die soon.

Cairo moved restlessly against him. He pulled away. "Would you touch me, Daddy? I ache between my legs."

Yep. He would be dead in the next few minutes. "Flip around so I can rub it and make it better."

Cairo gingerly did as told, as if afraid he would move too quickly. The moment he was settled, he went back to sucking just the tip of Rhodes' dick.

Rhodes petted Cairo's erection and massaged the spot between his balls and asshole. His entire focus was on what Cairo did. The suction was just enough to make him crazy, but not enough for him to get off.

"Can I tell you a secret?"

Rhodes nearly groaned at the whispered question. Each word brushed against his desperate cock. Cairo would for sure be the death of him. "Of course, baby."

"I like putting my pacifier in my butt. Don't tell, okay?"

Rhodes swallowed hard again. If this didn't end soon, he might do anything. Truthfully, Rhodes wasn't that big into the age-play aspect of this dynamic, but he adored caring for his boy, and Cairo was sexy as fuck. "I won't. You should do that now."

Cairo scrambled up the bed like he couldn't wait.

Rhodes rummaged through the bedside table for the lube and a condom. All pretenses of play fell away. Cairo's tongue was in his mouth while Rhodes fought to put on a condom.

Cairo grabbed the lube and readied himself.

Rhodes breathed like he had already run a marathon. Cairo had him that ready to go. When Cairo finally sank onto Rhodes' dick, a sound like a dying man fell from Rhodes' lips. His entire body reacted. Chill bumps rose on his skin. For a moment, Cairo held still, as if adjusting to the intrusion. Then he lifted and lowered himself again. Cairo whimpered. That sound alone nearly made Rhodes blow. He ground his back teeth to stop himself from ruining everything.

"Please, Daddy. My private parts are throbbing. I need to make it spit."

Rhodes rolled and pinned Cairo beneath him. All hints of softness had gone from him. He used Cairo. His tight asshole was all Rhodes cared about. He thrust and pumped. Cairo was so tiny, he was easy to treat like a toy, taking what he wanted. Still, he managed to follow the sounds Cairo made to keep his angle where Cairo enjoyed himself too. He wouldn't be satisfied until he made Cairo's body dance. He wanted to feel that asshole try to suck him deeper.

Cairo's short fingernails scraped his arms. He took it like a man who loved getting dicked down. Cairo writhed beneath him, looking like the hottest porn.

"That's it, baby. Take it. I want to watch you come."

Cairo whimpered. He visibly strained to reach the edge.

Rhodes wouldn't make it much longer. He reached between them and tugged Cairo's erection.

Cairo's back bowed. His moans turned rhythmic while Rhodes gave him everything. Sweat poured down Rhodes' spine. Cairo cried out. Cum filled the space between them. Rhodes lost it. He slammed himself into Cairo over and over until the pressure finally turned to ecstasy. Too late, Rhodes realized he didn't make a sound. He simply stared at Cairo with all the intensity in his soul. Cairo stared back. He had never felt more connected to anyone in his life. What in the fuck was he supposed to do now?

Chapter Two

DAYLIGHT POURED THROUGH THE windows. Birds chirped outside. The sensation of eyes on him had Rhodes sitting upright with his gun aimed at the face above him. His boss, and Beau's righthand man, Henry, didn't look the least bit moved by having a weapon leveled at him.

"Get dressed. Beau wants to see you downstairs."

Rhodes blinked at the hard tone. As far as he knew, Henry had no beef with him. Rhodes always did his job. “Yeah. Okay.” He swiped his hand over his face, trying to clear the cobwebs from his mind. “Give me a second and I’ll head down.” His gaze slid toward the spot next to him. It was empty. Disappointment poured through him. Of course, Cairo was gone. What did he expect? He was incapable of keeping anyone. Rhodes was too intense. He probably scared the hell out of Cairo. The guy had undoubtedly run the moment Rhodes fell asleep. Rhodes would do the same in his shoes.

Henry left him to dress.

Rhodes tried not to look at the empty bed. Cairo could have stayed. He didn’t need to go back to hiding at The PlayPen. Banks was Beau’s son. Beau would take

Cairo in if he asked. Cairo didn't need to be in Rhodes' bed. Rhodes would rather Cairo be safe than anything. If that meant pretending last night never happened, then so be it. Cairo was too sweet to live in fear. Maybe he would talk to Beau about it after their meeting. He was curious as hell to know what had happened. Henry had sounded serious. Beau didn't have big meetings with him unless something huge went down. Rhodes needed to focus on anything other than that empty bed while he got ready. Fuck. His chest hurt. It had only been a simple night of fun. He was being ridiculous. Rhodes massaged his sternum on his way downstairs. He had so many questions. Likely, he would never know the answers. For whatever reason, he hadn't been good enough. Maybe he had been too rough.

Damn. That was probably it. This was exactly why he needed to avoid the power dynamics. He was a greedy fuck. Cairo was too sweet for all that.

Rhodes' feet slowed as he reached Beau's office. His eyes automatically found Cairo. He sat in the corner, tucked beneath Beau's husband's arm. They were both dressed like bunnies. Cairo's nose and eyes were red. Tears streamed down his face while he sucked furiously on a pacifier. Kylo patted him and tried to comfort him. Cairo looked too trapped in his own terror to notice.

Rhodes tore his gaze away. He automatically focused on Beau. Beau's deadly ice-blue eyes watched him cross the room. He looked harder than Rhodes had ever seen him, and that said a lot. While he couldn't imagine Beau terrorizing Cairo, something definitely had, and Beau was the deadliest thing in the room.

Beau motioned toward an empty chair across from him at his desk. Rhodes immediately sat. A terrible sense of foreboding rose inside him. He had no clue what was happening, but it obviously wasn't good. Beau motioned toward Henry. Henry moved from his spot as Beau's sentry and handed Rhodes a piece of paper.

"This came by messenger this morning."

At Beau's claim, Rhodes' gaze shot around the room once more before dropping to the letter. Once he started reading, all he knew was rage. All he saw was red.

You have something that belongs to me. I expect him returned unsullied. While I know you had nothing to do with him turning up on your doorstep, I still expect Cairo to be sent home immediately. I apologize for any inconvenience he's caused you. He'll be properly disciplined for any disruption he's caused to your household. I should've put him down a long time ago, but I've had too much of a soft spot for him. Make sure he understands how upset I am for his behavior. He might've survived the last time I tried to kill him. I doubt he will twice.

My apologies and sincerely,

Hugh Freight

All Rhodes saw were the scars that littered Cairo's torso. There was nothing else in his head. Hugh Freight. That motherfucker. Rhodes knew him. Everyone on this side of the law knew each other. Though he doubted Hugh Freight was the guy's real name. But Hugh never crossed paths with Beau for a reason. Hugh worked the sex-trafficking game and Beau didn't touch that shit. People like them minded their business, no matter how distasteful they found each other. This was different, though. He knew Beau hated abusers, but this was stepping on the toes of another crime boss. Beau was a cold bastard. He could always go either way on any topic, especially since harboring Cairo might mean starting a war.

Rhodes ran his tongue over his teeth, trying to hold back his temper as he set the letter aside. He didn't want Beau to see the rage boiling inside him when he met Beau's stare.

Unfortunately, Beau watched him a little too closely. The guy saw everything. Of course, he wouldn't come right out and say as much. "Last night's security detail tells me you're the one who brought Cairo here."

Rhodes gave him a sharp nod. He was curious as hell to know how Cairo went from being in his bed to wearing a pair of Kylo's pajamas and crying in the corner. He didn't think he would like the answer.

Beau leaned back in his chair. His expression turned a little too businesslike. Rhodes had a bad feeling he would be the one making things right with Hugh. "Do you plan to take care of him?"

Rhodes' mood swung wildly. He almost laughed aloud at Beau's question. He sounded exactly like a parent, giving a stern lecture on taking care of the stray he brought home. “Yes.”

“You do understand what that entails, right? I won’t let this house be endangered.”

Rhodes got it. If Cairo wanted to leave, he wouldn’t do so alive. Rhodes would have to kill him if he didn’t want him. It wouldn’t take long for Cairo to have seen too much in this house. “I understand.” God, he didn’t know if he could hurt Cairo. It was more likely he signed his own death warrant.

Beau released a loud sigh and sat forward. “Henry, pick your team. Make sure Hugh understands Cairo is ours and what happens when he threatens one of mine.”

Henry didn’t hesitate. He headed for the door. “On it.”

Beau shuffled some papers on his desk. “Take your man and go. He needs comforting.” Beau didn’t look at him as he gave the order.

Rhodes hid a smile. Beau might be a lot of things, but he was also a daddy. Kylo was his world, and he took damn good care of him. He would expect the same of Rhodes and wouldn’t allow Hugh to ever touch him again. If Cairo chose him, Rhodes would treat him like a king. He prayed Cairo made that choice. The alternative was unthinkable. He felt sick.

Cairo was a wreck. He had woken up starving. After finding one of Rhodes’ huge t-shirts, he had gone in search of food. The sound of music had carried him to a playroom where an adorable bunny had been dancing. Kylo had spotted Cairo watching and immediately befriended him. The next thing Cairo had known, Kylo had him in matching pjs and a tea party was underway. They had hazelnut crepes. Cairo had felt so warm and at home. Then that letter had arrived. Embarrassingly, he had been inconsolable since. Kylo had shoved a pacifier into his mouth and done his best to comfort Cairo. But the thought of being forced back to Hugh had taken out his sanity. He didn't understand how Hugh had found him. Cairo had been at The PlayPen for days without being discovered. He didn't fully grasp what was happening, but he knew the pain would come soon. This time, he likely wouldn't survive.

He watched Rhodes talk to Beau. No words penetrated his panic. Rhodes looked so closed—like he hated Cairo now. Then Rhodes crossed the room and scooped Cairo into his arms. Cairo cried harder. It was nice to be held so lovingly, and soon that would end. There was no way Rhodes could understand what their one night together had done for him. He thought his chest would cave, thinking it would never happen again. Likely, nothing good would happen to him ever again. He had narrowly survived the last time Hugh had taken his anger out with a blade. Only the fact that Hugh liked it when he struggled and cried had saved him then. Of course, Hugh had watched him bleed out for a second before bringing in his surgeon. That was the day Cairo had started his plan to escape. Freedom had been embarrassingly short-lived.

Rhodes carried him back to bed with a muscle jumping in his jaw. He sat next to Cairo with his back against the headboard. Rhodes stared straight ahead. Finally, he met Cairo's stare, and Cairo saw the hurt in his eyes. "Did Beau catch you when you tried to sneak away? You could've told me thanks for one night, but no thanks. I'd never hurt you. I would've driven you back to the club."

Cairo had never been more confused. That was saying something, considering his entire life had been a mess. Cairo plucked the pacifier from his mouth. "Why do you think I tried sneaking away?" Nothing could have pulled him from his meltdown faster.

"You were gone when I woke up." It couldn't have been more obvious he hid his hurt behind a brick wall.

Cairo had to fix it. "I got hungry."

Rhodes visibly deflated. "I should've fed you before bed last night. Sorry. Guess I kind of suck at being a daddy."

Cairo swiped at his face. It was time for him to be a big boy. He climbed onto Rhodes' lap. "I know I'm a mess, but that's not your fault. Please don't be sad."

Rhodes wrapped his arms around Cairo and snuggled him. "I'm not sad. I'm fucking pissed. You have no idea how much I want to go beat the life out of Hugh." Cairo felt Rhodes' muscles relax. He looked guilty. "I guess I am a little sad too. When you popped up in my life last night, it was just in time to save me from drowning." The discomfort in Rhodes' voice sounded like embarrassment over baring a weakness. "Now I know how badly you've been hurt, and I realize you deserve to be free. You definitely don't deserve to be stuck with me, or need another daddy, especially one as moody as I can be."

Cairo wasn't the Little now. He was a terrified man who'd had one amazing night and now watched it slip away. "What are you saying?"

Rhodes didn't meet his stare. "There are plenty of rooms around here. I think you should pick one of them and restart your life. It sounds like you've been through a lot. If you choose to stay with me, you'll come out the other side of this one of these days and see me as dead weight. You'll see me as the person keeping you from your freedom. I want better for you than me."

Cairo couldn't believe his ears. It was as if Rhodes didn't see him at all. "I watched you for days before approaching you." It was hard for Cairo to admit that, but he honestly believed Rhodes needed him too. "Admittedly, one reason it took me so long is because you were always surrounded by other daddies. I was too embarrassed to approach you with witnesses. But mostly, I was just in observation mode. I saw the way you looked at other couples, and I thought, 'He sees it too. He sees the way everyone else has more, and their relationships don't look like my life with Hugh.' I chose you." Cairo realized he made himself sound like the prize with that confession, but he knew Rhodes understood what he meant. They were alike. Cairo had chosen the one person in that club who needed love as much as he did.

"Did you find something to eat?"

A smile snapped to Cairo's lips at the way Rhodes still thought of only him. "Kylo fed me."

Rhodes nodded. "He'll make a great playmate for you." He visibly hesitated. "That is, if you're staying."

Cairo was scared to hope. "What about Hugh? He doesn't really want me, but he won't let me go. I'm dead if he gets his hands on me. He'll hurt you to get to me."

"Beau is handling it. As long as you're part of Beau's household, he won't let anything happen to you. I won't let anything happen to you."

Cairo licked his lips in his nervousness. He wasn't good at having adult conversations. Life was so much simpler when he got to play the baby. "Are you asking me to stay? With you," he clarified, since Rhodes had said part of Beau's household. Rhodes hadn't said his household. He had a bad feeling Rhodes still meant to set him free.

"Yes." Zero hesitation. Full eye contact. Steady voice. Rhodes meant that shit. He wanted Cairo.

Cairo needed Rhodes to understand he meant this shit too. "I'd like that. The staying with you part." He over thought for a second. "And the playing with Kylo part too. We had a tea party with his bear friends." Excitement filled Cairo the more he spoke. He bounced a little on Rhodes' lap. "Did you know Kylo is a ballerina? Like, for real. He was on stage and everything. Of course, I don't know if they call men ballerinas, but he's a very pretty princess, so it fits."

The way Rhodes smiled filled Cairo with so much hope for the future, he thought he would explode. "He has an extremely famous mom too. You'll meet all types here. We're an eclectic bunch."

He was really serious. Rhodes wanted to keep him. Cairo had begged the universe so hard for a savior. He had pleaded for a real daddy for him and only him. Not a man he had to share who didn't need an excuse to abuse him the way Hugh had. Yeah, he understood that was some full-on Stockholm syndrome shit, but things were how they were. He had given up hope this life would find him. Realistically, he understood Rhodes could turn out to be just like Hugh, but Cairo doubted it. Rhodes was too much like him: starved of love.

“What should we do first?”

A huge grin spread across Rhodes’ face. “If you’re staying, you’ll need some clothes and toys.”

A wave of sadness washed over Cairo. “I had to leave everything behind when I ran.”

Rhodes kissed the tip of his nose. “Don’t worry. I’ve got you. I’ll give you a good life.”

Cairo knew that. He had seen all the bad and evil. Rhodes was the opposite of all that. That was exactly why Cairo had picked him. He looked like someone Cairo could love.

Chapter Three

Even after hours of shopping alongside Cairo and Kylo, Rhodes' insides still shook. Too much had happened too quickly. He adored Cairo's smile. His bright blue eyes swam with happiness, and Rhodes needed him to stay that way. Occasionally, a too-loud voice or noise would send Cairo scurrying beneath Rhodes' arm. Rhodes' protective personality and his possessiveness kicked in every time. The possessive part didn't make sense, honestly. They didn't know each other. Maybe Rhodes would be the one who wanted out. At the thought, his gaze automatically latched onto Cairo.

As if he felt Rhodes' stare, Cairo's head turned. His innocent persona slipped. Cairo visibly undressed Rhodes with his eyes. The hair on Rhodes' arms stood. Yeah. The lust between them was real. Rhodes doubted he would tire of that.

However, the truth still loomed on the horizon. He knew all the way to his soul this budding new thing between them was temporary. Cairo didn't see it yet. He was blinded by relief. One day, probably sooner rather than later, Cairo would realize this second chance at life was one hundred percent real. When that happened, he would look around and see the bars of his cage. It was inevitable. When that time came, as long as Cairo didn't leave the family, Rhodes would set him free. Just the idea of watching Cairo look at someone else the way he did Rhodes had Rhodes' hands itching to squeeze the life from a hypothetical man. But Rhodes wouldn't do that when that day came. He would let Cairo embrace life the way he deserved—the way that had been stripped from him by Hugh. Rhodes felt sick.

Cairo headed his way, rubbing the sleeve of a fuzzy jacket against his cheek. "Feel this one."

Rhodes did his best to hide his black thoughts. He touched the sleeve. It felt like petting a rabbit. "That's not rabbit fur, is it?"

A horrified look passed over Cairo's face. "Oh, no." He checked the tag. Rhodes practically felt Cairo's relief. "Thank goodness. It's faux rabbit fur. I hate people who kill innocent things just because they can or think they can profit from being cruel."

Rhodes knew Cairo meant more than bunnies. The injustice practically dripped from him. Rhodes' chest tightened. He didn't know how to take away the demons in Cairo's head.

He took the jacket from Cairo. "I'll hang on to this. Go pick out whatever you want."

Cairo chewed his bottom lip for a second. His precious-looking eyes slid away from Rhodes' stare. "I don't have any money. You've already bought me all the clothes I need to survive. I feel bad enough for being a burden. You—"

Rhodes ran his finger along Cairo's jawline, enticing his focus back to Rhodes' eyes. He needed Cairo to understand his place in Rhodes' life. "You chose me to take care of you. That means I provide everything. Not just necessities, but everything. Get as much or as little as you genuinely want. I can more than afford it." While Beau taking Rhodes in had bought Rhodes' loyalty, the astronomical amount of money Beau paid him sealed the deal on Rhodes' place on Beau's team. That was without even mentioning the free room and board, access to any car he needed on property, and lavish gifts he received. Truthfully, Beau had rendered paying him damn near useless, so yeah. There was less than zero chance Cairo would break his bank.

Cairo chewed his bottom lip again. He shifted from foot to foot. Rhodes couldn't take it. He kissed Cairo, stopping the nervous tick. Cairo took a shaky-sounding breath and Rhodes knew he had won.

While cupping Cairo's cheek, Rhodes dragged his thumb across Cairo's bottom lip. "Go find more things that make you happy. I've got you."

Cairo slowly nodded. "Okay." The response was little more than a whisper and sounded sweet as hell.

Rhodes' fought the evil smile that threatened to ruin everything. "That's my boy."

Cairo returned to Kylo's side.

Rhodes' ego swelled. Yeah, they were still likely temporary, but Rhodes wouldn't shun the opportunity set in his path. Cairo needed a daddy. Rhodes wanted the job.

Cairo smiled and laughed more in one day than he ever had before in his life. Kylo was different than anyone Cairo had ever met. He was a free spirit. If Kylo felt like dancing in the middle of the store, he did. If he wanted to wear two different-colored shoes and bows in his hair, he did. Everyone smiled when he was around. While Cairo knew he would never feel as free as Kylo, he envied him. He was self-aware. Cairo knew there were parts of him that wouldn't heal. That was okay. Rhodes looked at him like there was no one he wanted more. That was the balm he needed.

Cairo had tried to be as frugal as possible. He hadn't owned a lot at Hugh's. Cairo was accustomed to going without. He could make three cheap outfits work. Rhodes had already surpassed that by a mile. Cairo had lost track of what he had been given. It made him feel awkward. They didn't know each other that well yet. Maybe all the gifts came with strings. Horrible strings. Every time Cairo had pointed out discount stores, everyone had ignored him and headed inside places that had guards blocking the door. It was as if everyone they encountered already knew Kylo and his bodyguards. Kylo always stopped and talked to the guards and asked about their families. He was kind. He made Cairo feel lacking in every way. Kylo was so many things. He seemed very adult at times. Steady. Strong. Cairo doubted he would ever be those things.

Warm lips touched his nape, making Cairo realize he had been staring at his feet while Kylo shopped. He didn't want to look around. Cairo was scared to want more. Goosebumps skirted his skin as those lips brushed him again.

"Why are you sad?"

Cairo's head shot up. He immediately turned. Cairo couldn't let Rhodes think that. "I'm not." As the denial left his lips, Cairo realized he would have to admit his feelings. Otherwise, Rhodes wouldn't believe him. Heat rushed to his face. Being a penniless slave was humiliating. Cairo didn't know how to be anything else.

"I know you told me to pick out whatever I want. It's harder than I expected. The more I have, the more I have to lose." It hit Cairo. Maybe he shouldn't have said that. It was possible Rhodes would punish him for disobeying. A knot formed in his stomach. He braced himself.

Rhodes kissed him.

Cairo still didn't relax. Kisses could be tricks sometimes. Rhodes was close enough to hurt him.

"Come with me." Rhodes took his hand. He motioned toward Kylo's guards, Mickey and Edge. Then he made another hand gesture Cairo didn't understand.

Cairo's pulse pounded in his ears. He understood what being pulled aside meant. Cairo tried his ass off not to hyperventilate. Then a bright store came into view. Everything was bubbly. Cairo forgot his fear. He tried looking in every direction at once. Cairo had been so lost in his fear, he hadn't realized a second guard followed on their heels. Rhodes headed inside the colorful business. There were toys and costumes for all age groups. Technically, they were squishy character pajamas, but he was certain the store advertised them as costumes.

Rhodes didn't wait for Cairo to explode with excitement. He grabbed a floppy stuffed dog and handed it to Cairo. "Take this."

Cairo's fingers automatically closed around the dog's foot. He couldn't contain his joy a second longer. A small squeak escaped him. "It's so soft." He hugged the dog against his chest.

Rhodes turned down an aisle. Cairo followed, walking slowly. He didn't know if he was supposed to follow. Rhodes grabbed a building block set and a really cool racetrack. He held them up. "Do you like race cars or building things? Both?"

"Race cars." Even Cairo heard the reluctance in his voice. He had no idea what was happening or how he was meant to respond.

Rhodes tucked the track under his arm and grabbed a few cars.

"I can carry those."

Cairo nearly jumped out of his skin at the man's voice behind him. Once again,

Cairo never got to go places. He wasn't used to having bodyguards surrounding him.

Rhodes passed the toys to the guy behind Cairo. His sexy eyes focused on Cairo. "What's your favorite toy?"

Cairo shrugged. "Until Banks took me in, I never had any."

Thankfully, Rhodes didn't seem to judge him. "Was there anything at The PlayPen you liked the most?"

"Puzzles."

Rhodes gave him a sharp nod and took his hand. Together, they found the puzzles. Rhodes picked up some baby puzzles. Cairo eyed the big boy puzzles with longing. He liked the pretty ones that let him forget for a while. When his mind was focused on digging through the pieces, he didn't have to think.

Rhodes put the baby puzzle back. He moved to Cairo's side. He pointed at a movie-themed box. "I like that one."

Cairo's gaze shot to Rhodes. "You do puzzles too?"

While still perusing the different designs, Rhodes didn't look his way. "Yeah. It's soothing, but I don't like them any smaller than five hundred pieces."

Cairo nodded. "Those are too easy. But I don't like anything more than fifteen hundred pieces."

Rhodes nodded. "Once they get too big, trying to find the pieces you need becomes more of an exercise in frustration.

It's supposed to relieve stress not cause it."

Cairo felt a connection fall into place. He liked Rhodes. Cairo didn't feel as alone as usual. He picked up a box with a dragon on it. "I like this one too."

Rhodes held his stare. "We should get both, don't you think?"

Knowing Rhodes wanted to play too eased the weight on his chest, setting him free. "Maybe we put the racetrack back and get the one that looks like a bowl of candy too."

Rhodes' sweet, genuine smile had Cairo falling under his spell. "You can get the racetrack too, or do you not really want the racetrack? You can be honest. I want to know the real you."

He didn't, but Cairo got the gist of his claim. "I like puzzles better than toys. They make me feel like a big boy."

While Rhodes didn't exactly eye him for too long, Cairo got the feeling his confession unlocked some knowledge inside Rhodes. If so, he didn't share. His gaze moved over Cairo's shoulder. "Do you mind putting those back?"

"On it."

Rhodes' gaze moved back to hold his stare. "What about the dog? Does he make you feel too little?"

Cairo looked down at the dog. He still had it crushed against him. No matter what he tried, Cairo couldn't force his arms to let go. "He's a good dog." Even Cairo heard the way his voice broke. He didn't want to leave the dog behind.

Rhodes set the puzzles they had chosen aside and crowded Cairo's space. Cairo didn't try to get away. He wasn't scared. Rhodes' expression didn't scream anger. His expression was something totally different. Cairo didn't know what he saw, but he liked the way Rhodes made him feel. He cupped Cairo's face and kissed the tip of his nose. "If anyone tries to take that dog from you, I'll kill them."

He would. Cairo heard the truth behind every word. "Thank you." He couldn't speak above a whisper. Cairo couldn't let anyone else see how safe Rhodes made him feel. Maybe they would try to take him away.

"Come on, guys. We're getting ice cream."

Cairo's ears perked up. He looked Kylo's way. "There's ice cream?"

Kylo spun in place as if he tried to make himself dizzy. “Yep. I just have to make sure I don’t accidentally get anything soy. That almost killed me once.”

Kylo stopped spinning. He didn’t look disoriented at all. “On the other hand, Daddy stayed in bed with me afterward.”

“Don’t even think about it,” Mickey growled behind.

Kylo winked and walked away. For the very first time in his life, Cairo dared to hope.

Chapter Four

RHODES HADN'T STOPPED THINKING about Cairo's confession all day. He liked feeling like a big boy. There was a sick feeling deep in his gut. He didn't know how to prove his theory. But the clothes Cairo chose and the toys he wanted had something just on the edge of his brain, waiting to become a horrible revelation. All Rhodes could do was keep pushing forward.

After climbing out of the shower and drying off, he helped Cairo out of the tub and scrubbed him dry with a towel. "After we left the mall, I happened to think we didn't get you anything to relax in or sleep. Fletch volunteered to go back and grab a few more things."

Cairo looked as if he bit back the temptation to argue. It was obvious he really didn't like Rhodes buying him things. Cairo would have to suck it up. This was his new life. "He didn't have to do that. I don't need anything."

Rhodes ignored Cairo's objections. He led Cairo to the bed where a selection of freshly laundered pajama options waited. "Everything has already been washed. It's not like we can take anything back."

He watched Cairo openly fight with himself. "I guess that makes sense. There's no sense in letting anything go to waste."

"Exactly." Cairo would never win this argument. It was Rhodes' money. He would do as he pleased. "He didn't know what you liked, so he bought a bunch of different stuff."

Rhodes held his breath as he watched Cairo gingerly pick through each outfit. There were two pairs of onesies, two pairs of pajama sets with fire trucks and dinosaurs, and then there were three pairs of adult pajama pants along with some simple white t-shirts. Cairo rubbed the adult pants between his fingers, testing the softness. Rhodes realized he did that a lot. He seemed to be a tactile person.

"Those would look really good on you. They're the same color as your eyes."

A smile exploded across Cairo's face. "I don't have gray eyes, silly. They're blue. That's what Hugh ordered." Cairo made the claim so casually. Rhodes wasn't even sure if Cairo realized how much he exposed with that one statement. Rhodes had a hard time keeping his rage in check. He needed to stay calm and nonchalant. Otherwise, Cairo would withdraw.

"How old were you when you went to live with Hugh?"

Cairo shrugged. "I was too young to remember." He brushed the pants across his cheek. "Do you really think I could wear these?"

Rhodes could barely breathe or think. “Absolutely.” Who was that calm person answering questions? Rhodes wasn’t the least bit serene. He needed to kill someone. Unfortunately, he couldn’t tonight, and he needed to help Cairo find himself. “Try them on.”

Cairo dropped his towel. He was all excited smiles as he pulled the pants on. Rhodes handed him a shirt. Once Cairo was dressed, Rhodes took his hand and led him to a nearby full-length mirror. “Look at you. All grown up.”

Cairo twisted the hem of the shirt at Rhodes’ words.

Rhodes didn’t give up. He took a step back and raked Cairo’s body with a hungry gaze. Damn, he had a great ass. He met Cairo's gaze in the mirror. "Sexy as fuck."

Cairo's expression shifted. He transformed into the adult Rhodes now realized he wanted to be. "Does that mean you still want me like this?" There was the grown man Cairo actually was. He wasn't hiding now.

"I'd want you if you were in a burlap sack or a three-piece suit." He molded against Cairo's back and skimmed his lips across the spot beneath Cairo's ear. "I have a confession to make."

Cairo shifted from foot to foot.

Rhodes ran his hand down Cairo's body. "Last night, you tempted the fuck out of me. You found me in just the right headspace to take advantage of you. I shouldn't have done that."

"I—"

Rhodes kept talking, refusing to hear Cairo lose confidence. "You deserved for me to get to know you. I can't change that, but I want to know you. If that's dressed like this or however you want, you're still the person who saved me while I silently spiraled."

Cairo turned in his arms. "Are you saying you don't want to touch me again because you don't know me?" He looked like he was on the edge of tears.

A sad smile tugged at Rhodes' lips. "I'm saying I want you to choose me because you actually want me. The real you that no one else sees. I can't know you're only in my bed because you feel like that's the price you have to pay." Rhodes swallowed. It hurt. His voice exposed his pain. "I'm not Hugh."

It was likely the wrong thing to say, judging by the instant rage that flashed in Cairo's eyes. "So you think I'm a whore. Got it."

Rhodes held on to Cairo so he wouldn't run, even though he looked more likely to punch Rhodes. "For fuck's sake. I'm trying to say this is real. I want you for real."

Cairo's features softened. He shuffled closer. Suddenly, he looked vulnerable but not weak. "Do you have any idea how many powerful men walk through the door at The PlayPen? I know you do. But do you know how many of them offered to outright buy me? Most knew I belonged to Hugh. Worse, they knew how I came to belong to Hugh in the first place. You never approached me. In fact, you always looked right through me. You didn't see me until I sat in front of you. It was obvious you had no idea who I was. There's no way you don't know my head is a ten-car pileup with maximum casualties with little hope for survivors. But you don't look at me like you see any of that." Cairo's hands smoothed up Rhodes' chest before linking behind Rhodes' neck. He shuffled even closer, making it harder for Rhodes to breathe properly. "You have no idea how that makes me feel. I've never had anyone want me for me. No one has ever looked at me as human at all. I see you trying, and you'll never understand how much that means to me." He swiped his lips across

Rhodes' mouth. "It's sexy and makes me warm all over. So, yeah, it's you I want."

Despite his best efforts to not attack Cairo like it was the job that paid him, he took the kiss he wanted. Cairo didn't hold back either. His hands moved back to Rhodes' chest. He toyed with Rhodes' nipples.

Rhodes tore his mouth away and bit a path down the side of Cairo's neck. Something had been unleashed. A realization had formed that changed the trajectory of his life.

He pushed one side of Cairo's pants down one hip. Heat radiated between them. "Is it okay if we set the Little games aside for a while?"

Cairo's shaky breath assaulted Rhodes' ears. He sounded so aroused, Rhodes fought the urge to take him right there. “Please? I want that.”

There it was. The answer he already knew in his heart. Cairo wanted to be allowed to be an adult. Thank God.

Cairo was turned on, nervous as hell, and flying free all at once. Rhodes didn’t want to play games. Cairo couldn’t even begin to express how badly he wanted that too. He didn’t know if he felt safe enough to embrace a full-time adult role in life. Maybe Rhodes didn’t want someone who couldn’t be a boy sometimes. Cairo was still terrified of everything around him. But when Rhodes and he were alone, Cairo had never felt more grown in his life. The problem was, Cairo had no idea how to behave if he wasn't just someone's boy. Judging by the way Rhodes tore at his clothes, he must be doing something right. Something inside him got bigger. It felt a hell of a lot like courage.

He tore the towel from Rhodes' waist. His fingers encircled Rhodes' erection. That was for him. Cairo wasn't playacting, and Rhodes still wanted him. There was no faking his hard cock.

"I want you inside me." Cairo shoved Rhodes toward the bed.

Fuck... Rhodes' face. His expression. The hunger. Goddamn. Power rose inside him as Rhodes walked backward to the bed. His intense gaze never wavered. Cairo fought his way out of the clothes already hanging off him. They came together violently as they fell into bed. Cairo had no idea who dominated whom. He didn't care as long as Rhodes fucked him hard.

In their fight to be closer, Cairo ended up on top, taking what he wanted exactly the way he wanted the dick. He didn't care how he looked. Cairo was desperate for something Rhodes gave him. This new power likely had a name. Maybe it was something he wasn't ready to look at too closely. But Cairo was in charge, and he set the pace. In fact, Cairo didn't even know if Rhodes enjoyed himself at all. The only thing that mattered was taking his orgasm. No rules. No games. Just pleasure. Rhodes cried out beneath him. Cairo dropped his chin and savored the sight. Rhodes was muscular and strong. Cairo had him in his palm at the moment.

The pleasure won, holding his entire focus. Cum shot through the air before painting Rhodes' chest. It was the hottest sight Cairo had ever witnessed. As the last wave hit, only the sound of heavy breathing filled the air. Cairo couldn't stop looking into Rhodes' eyes as a slow realization formed. He wanted a real, loving relationship with Rhodes, and that looked unlike anything he expected.

Chapter Five

WITH HIS TONGUE HELD between his teeth, Cairo did his best to keep all his colors inside the lines. Meanwhile, Kylo brushed strokes across a canvas. Cairo couldn't see what he painted, but Kylo looked intense. No matter how hard he tried to lose himself in the activity, Cairo's mind kept returning to the night before. The way Rhodes had looked at him kept butterflies in his stomach. Cairo had been desired before, but things were different with Rhodes. The way Rhodes looked at him felt good. Natural. Healthy. The way Rhodes held him afterward still made Cairo glow with happiness. He didn't want to find a corner to hide in. Cairo hadn't felt that way yet with Rhodes. Without question, he was safe. It was an addictive feeling.

The hair stood on the back of Cairo's neck. He glanced up in time to see Rhodes walk away from the open door. A black t-shirt strained against his muscular body. He wore a gun like he came equipped with it. Cairo should be scared, knowing who he was and what he did. He wasn't. Rhodes was who he needed. Strong yet gentle. The desire to chase after him bordered on desperation.

"You look adorable in big-boy clothes." Kylo's words had Cairo's eyes swinging his way.

"Do you really think so?" The question popped out before Cairo had time to think. He ended up sounding a little too excited.

Kylo eyed him. He gave Cairo a sharp nod. "I do. You need a pop of color, though."

Cairo glanced down at himself. He wore blue jeans and a blue shirt. "Oh. I'm sorry. I didn't know." A pit opened in Cairo's stomach. He had tried something new and obviously had done it wrong. Cairo kind of thought he might hyperventilate. Everything he did was wrong. He didn't know how to please people.

Kylo stood. "Don't be silly." He grabbed Cairo's hand and pulled him to his feet. The overenthusiastic tug had Cairo nearly landing on his face. Somehow, he kept up.

"Where are we going?"

"To play dress-up, of course." Kylo made the statement like he thought Cairo could read his mind.

"Oh."

Kylo pulled Cairo into a room that was nothing but clothes. Puffy tutus and brightly colored tops sat alongside elaborate dresses and short costumes. Cairo tried looking in every direction at once.

Kylo pulled a bright purple silky vest from a hanger. "Here." He dressed Cairo while Cairo stood like a doll for his whims. Kylo buttoned the piece and took a step back. He tapped his chin. "Hmm. That's pretty good, but I can do better. Let's do this." He took the vest off and found a white Hawaiian shirt with bright orange flowers. Kylo tucked Cairo's arms into the holes but left it unbuttoned. With that done, he grabbed a brown fedora. After popping that onto Cairo's head, Kylo dragged Cairo to a vanity area at the opposite end of the closet. He shoved Cairo into a chair with his back to the mirror. Kylo hummed as he dug through a set of small drawers. He came out with something furry and small, but Cairo couldn't tell what it was. Kylo toyed with it for a second, peeling off a paper backing before tossing the trash over his shoulder.

"I can't wait for you to see this." Kylo chuckled and danced in place while pulling and tugging at Cairo's face. Then he suddenly spun the chair, leaving Cairo staring into the mirror at a stranger.

Cairo leaned closer. His mind didn't make a sound. A fake five o'clock shadow covered the lower half of his face. Between the hair, the hat, and the shirt, Cairo looked thirty. He couldn't stop looking at himself.

"Wow."

Kylo tapped his fingertips together and bounced in place. "Is that a good wow or a bad one? We can find something else."

"I can't believe I'm looking at myself, but it's a good wow. It's like I'm all grown up."

Kylo sat next to him on a bench built into the wall. "You are grown. That's the wonderful thing about being an adult. You get to choose. No one is the boss of you. You can wear this or even a dress. If you're feeling like you need extra comfort, then you can be a baby. I still get to wear my tutus like I'm on stage again. Every day, you can be someone new. You can be the old you or a new version you built. There's no reason you can't be something in between or something entirely different. You're free here."

Cairo went back to staring at his reflection. He wasn't sure he was ready to be quite this grown, but he also didn't want to be a baby today. While still staring into the mirror, he looked at the selection behind him. Something deep black caught his attention.

Cairo turned and pointed. "What's that?"

Kylo bounded to his feet. He pulled the material off the hanger. "Yes!" It was a short-sleeved button-down shirt.

Cairo was immediately on his feet. "I love it." The material was satin, and it caught the light. Cairo couldn't stop giggling as he changed shirts. The moment he was dressed, he automatically grabbed the neon purple vest he had discarded earlier. He was almost giddy as he shed the facial hair and hat.

Kylo sprang forward and ran his fingers through Cairo's hair, giving him a messy-hair look. He also unbuttoned the top few buttons on the shirt.

"That's your look."

Cairo nearly jumped out of his skin when Kylo's personal bodyguard, Mickey, spoke. He had been so quiet, Cairo forgot he was there. Cairo tried to cover his reaction.

He brightened. Before he could respond, Kylo dragged Cairo back to the vanity. This time, he didn't have to dig quite as much before coming back with makeup. He painted Cairo's eyes, giving them a smoky look that made the light blue color pop.

He saw Mickey nod behind him in the mirror. "Perfect. Rhodes will love it."

Cairo's gaze shot to hold Mickey's stare. "Do you really think so?"

Mickey nodded. "You should go see for yourself." He checked his watch. "He's probably hanging out in the security building right now. This is when he gives Teddy a lunch break."

Cairo exchanged glances with Kylo.

Kylo shooed him toward the door. "Go. Report back, though. I'm dying to know how he reacts."

Cairo stood. He twisted his fingers. "Okay." He took a step toward the door before freezing in place. "I don't know where the security building is."

Mickey waved for him to follow. "Come on. I'll get a guard to escort you."

He followed Mickey to the door. A guard leaned against the wall outside. Cairo realized he knew him. Fletch had been the guard at the toy store with him.

"Hey, Fletch. Can you walk Cairo to the security building?"

Fletch smiled. He looked nice. "Sure. Come on." His smile was sweet. That helped a little with the idea of being with such a huge stranger.

The idea of Rhodes seeing him dressed like this still stretched Cairo's nerves, though. "Hold on." He raced back to the coloring table and grabbed his stuffed dog. Cairo tucked him under his arm before jetting back to Fletch. "Okay. I'm ready."

Fletch's smile grew as they fell into step beside each other. As they made their way outside, Fletch focused on him. "You look nice."

Cairo flashed him a smile. "Thank you. I'm hoping Rhodes thinks so too. I'm not being his baby today."

Fletch shot him a confused look. "Why does that matter? I can't imagine that being something Rhodes cares about.

He's only dated one other Little before. Everyone else he's dated has been like me, I guess." He hesitated for a moment. "You know, just stuck being my real age."

Cairo practically felt the way Fletch tried to avoid using the word "normal." "What was he like?" He didn't know why he asked. Maybe he was into mental torment.

Fletch shrugged. "Who? Rhodes' ex?" He shrugged again and answered without waiting for Cairo to confirm that was who he meant. "If I'm honest, I never liked the guy. He was conniving. I don't believe he was as much of a Little as he was a user. All he did was take. It was kind of weird when he left."

"How so?" Cairo was invested now.

Thankfully, Fletch didn't seem opposed to gossip. "Rhodes was hurt, but he also didn't look anywhere near as pinched as he had with Brody. It was like a weight was lifted from his shoulders. I doubt Rhodes will admit it, but I don't think he was very happy in that relationship. Don't get me wrong, he loved taking care of Brody, but it was very one-sided. He deserves someone who wants to make him happy too." Fletch looked his way. "I can see how much his feelings matter to you. I'm glad he met you."

Cairo's face heated. He wasn't used to praise. Luckily, he didn't have to respond.

Fletch motioned toward a smaller house ahead. "That's the security building. Would you like me to walk you to the door?"

Cairo waved off the suggestion. “I’ll be okay.” Plus, he kind of needed a few minutes to clear his head. He couldn’t let Fletch think it was reflection of him. “But I really liked talking to you. Maybe we can talk again sometime.” Cairo had enjoyed the adult tea spilling. Plus, he just needed friends.

“I’d love that.”

With the promise of speaking again secured, Fletch headed back toward the main house. Cairo focused on where Rhodes worked. He took a deep breath and moved in that direction. Fletch was right. Rhodes needed someone who wanted to make him happy. That someone was Cairo. He held his stuffed dog tighter. He would make Rhodes feel like a king.

While Rhodes stared at the monitors at the security desk, he didn't see a thing. His mind was filled with nothing except for the way Cairo had looked at him after Rhodes kissed him goodbye for the day. There had been something in his eyes Rhodes had never seen before. He fought the urge to shirk his duties. There was something better he wanted to do.

A light knock tapped on the door. Rhodes' gaze snapped to that security camera feed. He shot to his feet. The camera didn't have a good angle. From what he could see, it wasn't anyone familiar. How had they gotten this far onto the property unnoticed? With his hand on his gun, Rhodes pulled open the door. Cairo stood on the other side, hugging his puppy like he was nervous as hell, and looking transformed. For a moment, Rhodes couldn't do anything but stare.

Cairo seemed to hug the dog tighter. "Are you going to shoot me?"

Rhodes shook his head, shaking the cobwebs loose. "What?" He realized his hand was still on his gun. Rhodes immediately dropped it. "No, baby. Of course not. You just caught me off guard. Come in." He backed up, giving Cairo space to step inside.

Cairo looked around. "Wow. This is super high-tech."

Rhodes couldn't think straight while looking at Cairo's painted eyes. "Yeah.

Um. It was designed by the best. You look different today."

"I've been playing dress-up with Kylo." That explained the blindingly bright vest.

Rhodes took Cairo's hand and moved to reclaim his seat. He pulled Cairo down to sit on his lap. "Which of you chose this outfit?"

"Me." He looked and sounded excited. "First Kylo tried to put me in a fedora and fake facial hair, but it didn't look like me. I picked the shirt and vest. Kylo did my eyes."

"You look gorgeous."

Cairo beamed with happiness. "I hope so. I really, really like this look. But I don't need to dress this way again if you don't want to look at me like this. I don't actually have to look at myself, so your opinion matters more."

He drove Rhodes crazy with the constant insecurities, but he understood where they came from. Rhodes didn't try to reassure him with words. He kissed him. Rhodes couldn't say what happened exactly. The new look might have turned him on, but their kiss was so sweet, the backs of his eyes burned. He could stay right there and kiss Cairo for the rest of his life and be content. Unfortunately, he was supposed to be working. As much as he hated giving up Cairo's mouth, he had to. Still, he kept brushing his lips lightly across Cairo's. "May I take you to dinner tonight?"

Cairo giggled. "So proper. Yes."

Rhodes couldn't stop smiling. The door opened, and Rhodes stood, lowering Cairo to his feet. He tried to look professional and not at all like he had been making out instead of working.

Teddy nodded to Cairo in greeting before focusing on Rhodes. "Thanks for the break. Henry wanted me to tell you to meet him in the garage."

That sounded a lot like bullshit was afoot. "Thanks. I'll head that way."

Rhodes escorted Cairo outside, doing his best to look like he was doing exactly what he was supposed to be doing.

Cairo broke the moment the door closed. "Oh, no. I didn't mean to get you in trouble or anything. Mickey said I should visit and show you my outfit. I didn't think about how it might look."

Rhodes squeezed his hand. "It's fine. I love having you around, and no one snitches in this house. Damn near all of us came from the streets and still live by street rules. As long as everyone stays safe and keeps the property secure, we're allowed to have lives."

Cairo nodded. "Okay. I don't want to be a nuisance here. You make me happy. I just want to make you happy too."

Rhodes couldn't stop the heated look he tossed Cairo's way. "Oh, I'm happy. You don't have to worry about that." There was no mistaking the heat in his claim.

Cairo blushed.

Rhodes headed for the back door, intent on walking Cairo back inside.

Henry stepped out of the garage before he made it. "Let's go." His hard, unforgiving tone said everything. It was about to be a long day, and they had no time to waste. Henry's humongous and goofy-as-hell husband, Field, bounded from the garage like an overenthusiastic puppy.

He linked arms with Cairo. "Come on. It's dancing time."

Cairo tossed him a confused look, but he let Field drag him away. As much as Rhodes wanted to make sure Cairo made it inside safely, he had to put business first or they wouldn't have a home.

Rhodes made sure he used his professional tone. "What's up?"

Henry motioned toward a black SUV. It was only one of the many vehicles on the property available for use to anyone. "Get in."

Rhodes didn't hesitate. He jumped into the passenger seat, matching the energy of Henry's tone. Things seemed serious.

Henry didn't enlighten him until they were on the road. "Hugh responded to our message. Grab that paper." Rhodes looked where Henry indicated with a nod. It was covered in blood. He gingerly unfolded it and read it out loud.

"This is how I deal with thieves. Bring back my property or I'll send another piece of him home every day I don't have Cairo."

Henry tossed a quick glance his way. "That came by messenger this morning along with James' hand."

Shit. He had hoped Hugh would recognize he was up against someone he couldn't beat and scurry back under his perverted rug. "Damn. I didn't mean for any of this to happen."

Henry's expression didn't so much as shift. "Did you know Cairo belonged to Hugh when you brought him home?"

"No."

Henry shrugged. "Then it's not on you."

He couldn't let Cairo take the blame either. "Cairo shouldn't—"

Henry cut him off. "You don't have to plead your man's case. I saw him when Hugh's first letter came. Plus, we all know damn well what Hugh is. I have no doubt Hugh acquired Cairo as a child through his sick trade. No one should be condemned to that. He deserves to heal. I know you'll give him that. But we can't let Hugh think he can harm one of ours. After we recover James, we'll have to make a big statement. I played too nicely last time, trying to prevent a war. That's why James got hurt. I won't make that mistake twice."

Rhodes nodded along to every word more for himself than Henry. They couldn't let James down, and Rhodes wanted to watch the life leave Hugh's eyes. Maybe it wouldn't be tonight, but Hugh's days were numbered. He could count on that.

Chapter Six

Rather than going to his room first, Rhodes borrowed Mickey's shower and a set of clothes. He couldn't let Cairo see him covered in blood. The house was silent. It had taken them hours to carry out a plan that created maximum damage with no risk to themselves. If Hugh forced their hands again, they would simply send in the Agafonov family to gut the entire organization. The Agafonov brothers were a group of trained assassins and spies Beau had brought to live with them. They were the most sought-after group in the country if someone needed to be killed. There was no one they couldn't reach. That was why it was good to have them on their side.

With the blood washed away, Rhodes headed for the room he now shared with Cairo. It was empty. Rhodes' brow furrowed as he searched every corner. He backtracked. Beau and Kylo had already retired for the night, so Cairo wouldn't be in the playroom. He ran into Fletch on the way down the stairs. Since Fletch was in pajamas and carrying snacks, Rhodes doubted he knew anything, but Rhodes had to ask someone.

"Hey, man. Have you seen Cairo?" Rhodes was surprised how friendly he sounded, considering he was terrified.

Something dark passed over Fletch's face. He took a few seconds before answering, as if he questioned if he should. "Last time I saw him, he was in the kitchen." Without another word, Fletch stepped around him and continued his way up the stairs.

Rhodes had no clue what he could have done to piss off Fletch. Unless he blamed Rhodes for James. Fuck. Sometimes there were no right answers. Rhodes practically jogged to the kitchen. He was a lot more worried than he cared to admit. Rhodes spent a lot of time expecting Cairo to disappear at any given moment. The thought scared the fuck out of him. When he burst into the kitchen and found Cairo sitting on a stool at the kitchen island, a tsunami of relief washed over him. For half a second, anyhow.

Then he took in the scene and his heart stopped. Cairo wore footie one-piece pajamas that looked like a dog. He tightly held his stuffie. The tip of his nose and his eyes were blood red. Tears flowed freely down his cheeks. He kept swiping his face on the stuffed dog's head as broken stuttered breaths left him. It was obvious he had been crying hard for a long time. A box of cereal and an unused bowl sat in front of him.

Rhodes was across the room in a flash. He wrapped his arms around Cairo. "Oh my god, sweetie. What's wrong?"

Cairo's entire body shook as he took a breath. "I waited for you for dinner."

Realization had his eyes falling closed. Goddamn it. He had asked to take Cairo out to dinner tonight. "Shit. I'm so sorry."

Cairo's voice got shakier, as if he hadn't hit the pinnacle of his breakdown yet. "Your hair is wet. You're wearing different clothes. I'm sorry I played dress-up and forced you to find someone else." He cried harder. "I swear I can be a good boy."

Something died inside Rhodes. This wasn't manipulation. Cairo genuinely believed he had chased Rhodes into someone else's bed. He one hundred percent thought he was bad, and Rhodes had punished him. He didn't know how to fix this.

Rhodes cupped Cairo's face and forced him to hold his stare. "There is no one else out there I want. You are everything to me and the only person who shares my bed. You're it for me. I showered and changed clothes so I wouldn't come to you covered in blood. When Beau or Henry tells me to jump, I don't have any other choice. But you never have to worry I'm out there cheating, because I'm not like that."

If Cairo believed him, Rhodes couldn't tell. When he looked at Cairo, all he saw was someone shattered. Rhodes didn't know how to fix anything. He never had. There was no way Cairo understood how badly Rhodes wanted to be his hero. Rhodes never got to be the good guy. With that depressing thought drowning him, Rhodes glanced toward the empty bowl. "Have you eaten anything yet?"

"There's no milk." Cairo started crying again, and Rhodes hated himself a little more. While Cairo didn't have a phone, so Rhodes could keep him posted, he could've stopped and texted any of the guys to pass along his message. He had genuinely forgotten their plans in the face of James' strife.

"Okay." Even to his ears, Rhodes sounded sad. "Let's do this." He took Cairo's hand and helped him off the stool. Rhodes dipped into Beau's office first and found the drawer filled with phones for anyone's use. They already had service. All Rhodes had to do was program the number into his phone and hand Cairo the device.

"Now, let's eat." Rhodes went straight to the garage, grabbed the first key fob he saw and strapped Cairo into the passenger's seat. In no time, they were off to a nearby fast-food place with car hops so they didn't even have to leave the vehicle. Nothing but silence filled the air.

Rhodes didn't ask what Cairo wanted. Cairo would probably pick a kid's meal—that wasn't enough food to feed a squirrel—just so he wouldn't burden Rhodes. There would be no more of that bullshit.

With their food ordered, he gave Cairo his full attention. He still hugged his dog with one arm and held the phone with his other hand. It hadn't occurred to Rhodes that Cairo likely didn't have pockets.

Rhodes took the phone and set the device in the console tray. "There. We'll get it when we get back home."

Cairo no longer cried, but his eyes still looked like a kicked puppy's. "You got me a big boy meal."

Rhodes didn't miss a beat. "That's because you're a big boy now. You need more food than a little kid."

Cairo nodded. "Okay."

The knowledge he hadn't gotten his chance to kill Hugh was a hot coal in his gut. "What happened to the makeup?"

Cairo's eyes slid away. "I took a shower and got ready for bed."

That was likely half true. But he had already inadvertently told Rhodes he thought Rhodes had found someone else because of that look. Rhodes was trying to reopen that line of communication. He couldn't let Cairo carry that mistaken belief in silence, letting that fear eat away at their relationship.

"I really am sorry I didn't find someone to deliver you a message. We were pretty focused on a problem that needed taken care of." He wouldn't tell Cairo anyone had gotten hurt because of him. Not being able to tell Cairo exactly what he had been doing—no doubt—added to Cairo's anxiety.

"You live at someone else's mercy. That's something I understand." Cairo absently toyed with a scar across his wrist Rhodes hadn't noticed before now. It broke his heart to think about how much Cairo had suffered. He deserved a soft life. Rhodes was determined that was exactly what Cairo would get.

Everything inside Cairo ached. He had been so happy this morning. Now he couldn't stop the black clouds that kept closing in on him. As they ate in silence, he felt the weight on his chest lift. A laugh escaped him after he ate his last fry.

A sweet smile popped to Rhodes' lips. "I love that sound. Do I get to hear the joke?"

Cairo warmed inside. He was so lucky to have Rhodes. Cairo hated the way the past undermined him. "I just realized I was more hangry than anything."

A huge grin split Rhodes' face. "That's okay. It happens to everyone."

Cairo made a helpless gesture. "I suffer a lot of food insecurity. At least I'm self-aware."

Rhodes wasn't smiling any longer.

Cairo really needed to learn when to stop talking. "Sorry." He mumbled the apology. No one wanted to hear about his trauma.

"Don't be sorry. I should fill the fridge and cabinets in the room. Since I usually grab food from whatever the family is eating, I don't keep much in the room."

"You have beer." Cairo knew that much. Searching Rhodes' room was the first thing he tried.

Rhodes grabbed the phone he had given Cairo. He clicked around for a few before setting the device aside again. "I just downloaded a food delivery app and signed you into my account. Since I already have a payment method saved, all you have to do is order whatever you want. They have restaurants and grocery stores to choose from. Just get whatever you want anytime you need. Hopefully, there won't be too many nights like tonight. Beau is about eighty percent retired, but he'll always have enemies. Thankfully, most people are too scared of his wrath to cross him. Every now and then, someone feels froggy again and tries him."

Cairo smiled. "Feels froggy? I haven't heard anyone say that in a long time."

They shared a glance and laughed. Cairo felt lighter. "I hate that it seems like I make your life harder every time you turn around. But I hope you know I like you a lot, and I really want to be with you." Cairo felt his cheeks heat. "Maybe I'm unlearning a lot of things, but I know you're amazing. Sometimes I just—" Cairo's hands rose and fell. He didn't know what he was trying to say.

Rhodes took Cairo's hand and brought it to his lips. The heat between them immediately cloyed the air. Cairo knew he was lacking in a million ways, but he fully intended to work his ass off to keep this.

"My life isn't harder. You've given me a reason to get up every day. There's no way you can know how much I need you in my life. You're all I think about. I can never get back to you quickly enough. You're under my skin."

God, he made Cairo feel things. He hadn't expected to live this long, much less find this amazing thing growing between them. He made Cairo strong and brave in ways he had never been before.

"I really want you to hold me."

At his confession, Rhodes kissed his hand again and then put the car in reverse. Cairo couldn't tear his gaze away. He didn't look to see where they went. It wasn't until Rhodes turned down a wooded road that Cairo noticed they weren't home.

Rhodes pulled over and grabbed a blanket from the back. "Come on."

Cairo climbed from the car, unsure of their destination. It didn't help that he wore footed pajamas and no shoes. He had to step gingerly.

Rhodes obviously noticed. He swept Cairo off his feet. "Don't worry. I've got you."

Cairo wrapped his arms around Rhodes' neck. He would go anywhere with Rhodes. A hammock came into view. It had the perfect view of the full moon. Rhodes climbed into the hammock with Cairo in his arms. He made it look easy, while Cairo had never mastered a hammock in his life. Not that he had been presented with many opportunities.

Rhodes covered them with the blanket.

Cairo stared at the moon. "It's beautiful here. Wherever here is."

Rhodes snuggled up like he planned to hold Cairo all night. "We're on Beau's land. It's just a secret little spot he carved out to spend time completely alone with Kylo. I doubt he plans to use it tonight." Rhodes kissed his ear, making chill bumps rise on his skin.

Cairo smiled at the sensation. Peace and happiness were all he knew. He couldn't stop himself from turning his head and capturing Rhodes' lips. Their kisses were slow and sweet. Cairo felt warm and fuzzy inside. Rhodes didn't try to seduce him or try for more at all. They just savored the way their lips felt when they touched. He wanted to spend his life right where they were. For the first time, the truth sank in. Rhodes, honest to God, didn't care what Cairo wore or what personality shone through day by day. He just wanted to be with Cairo. His eyes stung at the realization. For once, something really real was happening to him. It grew bigger with every passing moment. He wanted this. Whatever it took, Rhodes would always be his.

Chapter Seven

Cairo: *Would you like to have a tea party with me?*

Cairo: *Well, it's actually wine and cookies.*

Rhodes: *I'd love that. Just let me know where.*

Cairo: *Oh. Haha. I forgot that part. Our bedroom.*

Rhodes: *On my way.*

Rhodes: *Meet me in the garage. It's time for your first driving lesson.*

Cairo: *But my tummy hurts. Could you come rub it instead?*

Rhodes: *No fibs. No excuses. This is a skill you need.*

Cairo: *Okay*.

Rhodes: *No pouting either.*

Cairo: *sigh. I can't have anything.*

Rhodes: *What are you wearing?*

Cairo: *Button-down shirt and jeans. Why?*

Rhodes: *Just trying to decide how easily I can peel them off when you meet me in bed in five.*

Cairo: *I'll be nude before you get there.*

Rhodes: *Run*.

Cairo: *I just realized we've been together five months today.*

Rhodes: *I noticed that too. There's a gift on the bed for you.*

Cairo: *Squee!*

The ease with which they fell into a pattern of being together never ceased to blow Rhodes away. Cairo did his therapy sessions, and Rhodes joined him sometimes. Watching Cairo grow and heal was a balm to his soul. Everything about Cairo warmed his life. When they first met, Rhodes kept himself a little closed, fully expecting Cairo would get better and crave freedom. He was owed the ability to control his life and do what he wanted. Instead, his growth had moved him toward Rhodes. Not away. Rhodes couldn't pinpoint the exact moment it happened, but one day, he noticed he felt different. He believed in them. They were happy together. They equally wanted forever. There was no one Rhodes would rather be with. He felt like he had grown right alongside Cairo. Cairo was also just fucking beautiful. Rhodes had a terrible time keeping his hands to himself.

Cairo shifted.

Rhodes molded against his back and readjusted Cairo's stance. "You're shying away again. Believe in yourself. Take a breath." He listened to Cairo draw a steady breath. "Squeeze the trigger."

Cairo hit the target dead center. He threw his arms up in victory and bounced up and down. "Oh my God. Did you see that? I did that."

Rhodes guided Cairo's hand into a safer position. "I saw. Let's not forget you're holding a loaded weapon."

A nervous chuckle burst from Cairo. "Oh, right. Sorry. But did you see that?"

Cairo looked so adorable. While wearing a baggy T-shirt, jeans, and work boots, Cairo still managed to look dainty.

"I can't believe I'm good at this." The wonderment in Cairo's voice had pride growing in his chest.

"You master everything you touch." His belief in Cairo sounded in every word.

Cairo shuffled closer, looking like the cat that ate the canary. "Does that include you?"

Rhodes hauled Cairo against him. "That especially includes me." He held Cairo's hand with the gun away from them as he stole the kiss he wanted. While Cairo was really good at everything he did, he was also a bit of a klutz. He couldn't get enough of anything Cairo did.

"I wish I didn't have to work today." Rhodes whispered the confession between kisses. "I'd rather be with you."

He felt Cairo smile against his lips. "You can't get into trouble because of me. Go. I can clean up here."

With a groan, Rhodes took a step back. "Three more hours. I'll be done."

Cairo held his hand until the last second as Rhodes walked backwards away from him. The gesture filled his chest with warmth. He was totally in love with Cairo.

"Remember me." Rhodes said the words as dramatically as possible.

Cairo's laughing smile made everything brighter. "Goofball."

Rhodes covered his heart. "You wound me. I'm *your* goofball." He couldn't stop smiling.

"Mine." Even though Cairo still grinned like an idiot, his eyes flashed with hunger.

Rhodes shot forward and stole another kiss. He didn't know why he was so extra needy today, but he genuinely didn't want to leave. The desire to climb beneath Cairo's skin was massive. The door to the range opened. He forced himself away.

Fetch stuck his head in the door. "Come on. You know we have a meeting today."

Rhodes' gaze moved over Cairo's face. Emotions engulfed him. He swallowed them down. "I really have to go." Again, it took a second for Cairo to release his fingers.

"Dude, really? You're not headed for the gas chamber. Let's go."

Rhodes took a few more steps back, but he picked up the pace. "Love you. Don't get into trouble."

It took him a second to realize what he had said. The confession had rolled so naturally off his tongue. Rhodes didn't take it back. He simply jogged in Fletch's direction and out the door. Fletch genuinely looked irritated.

Rhodes hated that. "I'm sorry. I didn't realize the time."

Fletch's shoulders relaxed. He made a dismissive gesture. "Don't worry about me. I woke up in a pissy mood, and things have done nothing but gone downhill since. It's not on you."

Side by side, they walked toward the main house. "Do you want to talk about it?"

Fletch shrugged. "Banks handed me a seven-day ban from The PlayPen last night."

Rhodes' forehead furrowed. "What? Why? You're always super respectful."

"Sammie had a meltdown. I mean, really showed his ass. You know how he can be. Anyway, I finally hit my breaking point and screamed at him. Apparently, I frightened a bunch of Littles. Shit has gotten out of control with him. I just accepted my punishment and broke things off."

“Fuck.” Rhodes wouldn’t say he was sorry to hear it. Sammie was a real piece of work. Being a brat was one thing, but it was like the guy got off on humiliating Fletch in public. Rhodes had always hated him. “You two were together for a long time.”

Fletch tossed him a sad smile. “Yeah, but there’s a reason I never brought him here. In my heart, I knew we wouldn’t make it. He was fun, but life has been nothing but drama since we met. I want to find my peace—the way you have.”

A surprised bark of laughter burst from him. “Never in all my days would I have expected anyone to envy what I have. But yeah, that’s a good description. Cairo has had his dramatics, but he’s definitely my peace.”

Fletch nodded along. “I’ve never seen you the way you are with him. Maybe it’s just a case of the grass being greener. I should probably just apologize to Sammie.”

Rhodes did not like that plan. “Nope. You’re not doing that. When Banks lifts your ban, Cairo and I will go with you. We can be your buffer while you taste freedom.”

Fletch chuckled. “I’d like that. It used to be a lot of fun to hang out with the Littles before I let Sammie ruin my life. I don’t want to be the reason Sammie doesn’t have a safe place, but I also can’t let him steal any more joy from me.”

“Agreed.” They flashed each other a smile. Rhodes didn’t know if Cairo would want to step foot in The PlayPen again, but he knew Cairo cared about Fletch. They could be there for a friend. Rhodes had to think about anything other than dropping the L bomb on Cairo. He winced. Maybe he wouldn't think anything of it. Rhodes had wanted to have that conversation in a much more romantic setting. What if Cairo hadn't been ready to hear that? Rhodes hadn't considered that. Now, it was all he could think about. Damn, Cairo could be melting down right now, and Rhodes had to work. He already felt like three more hours on the schedule was soul-sucking. This was about to be the longest afternoon of his life.

Cairo had no idea how long he stared at nothing. He had heard Rhodes right? Surely Rhodes hadn't told Cairo he loved him. Obviously, Cairo loved Rhodes. He just hadn't found a way to have that conversation. A wave of nausea inexplicably washed over him along with the past.

The room kept getting darker around the edges. He desperately gasped for air each time Hugh's grip loosened on his throat.

"I want to hear the words, pet. It's your job to love me." He suddenly released Cairo's neck but not his hold on Cairo's body. His dark eyes were crazed. Cairo had seen this side of Hugh before. Nothing good would happen today. These moments were becoming more common than

not. It wouldn't be long until Hugh killed him. Cairo had gotten too old for him. Only nostalgia kept Cairo alive. That, and Hugh's sick obsession with breaking this one last thing inside Cairo. That was exactly why Cairo refused to say he felt something he never would. He was scared and in pain. Everything shook so hard, he felt sick. He ugly cried and couldn't stop. Cairo was definitely as pathetic as possible. He was a broken coward. Hell, he was just fucking broken. His sanity had fled long ago. He had never known pride. Cairo was a shattered mess with no hope. The only thing that still belonged only to him was his heart. He would die with that intact.

Hugh reached behind his back.

Cairo shook harder. Sheer terror had him in its grip.

"Say it, pet. Don't make me put you down like the useless dog you are."

Cairo couldn't have spoken even if he wanted to obey. His vocal cords had definitely been damaged this time. Cairo saw the end in Hugh's eyes as a punch landed in his midsection. He was right. It took him a second to realize the hit to his gut was actually a knife. He saw the blood covering the blade as Hugh lifted it to stab him again. Another blow to the chest.

"Please?" He had to push hard to force the word past bleeding lips.

"Oh, now you want to beg." He stabbed Cairo again. "You had your shot. This is on you."

Hugh didn't understand. Cairo didn't beg for his life. He pleaded for death. Cairo needed Hugh to end his life. That was the only way he would ever be free.

"Are you okay?"

Cairo blinked. An unfamiliar man stood feet from him. Cairo cleared his throat. "Yes, sorry." An embarrassed smile popped to his lips. "I guess I kind of spaced out there for a moment."

The guy nodded. "Yeah. I get it. You were pretty gone. I've been trying to get your attention for a minute."

Cairo fought a blush. He moved to the lockbox where Rhodes kept the gun he had bought for Cairo. For some reason, he couldn't let go of the weapon. "It seems like I'm a lot more tired than I realized." As the shock of the past faded, Cairo realized he was alone with a stranger. He licked his lips. His grip on the gun wouldn't loosen. The familiar sensation of being hunted for sport overcame him. "You don't look familiar to me." Cairo had to say something. He couldn't let the anxiety beat him.

"I'm James, but most everyone calls me JJ." He held out a bandaged arm with a missing hand. "Shit. Sorry. I keep forgetting." He switched hands.

Cairo lightly shook. "Cairo."

Something flashed across JJ's face, but he immediately hid his first reaction. Cairo had no idea what that was about.

"We've never met because I work a different shift than your man. Plus, I live in one of the houses farthest away from the main house. I've heard a lot about you, though."

A nervous chuckle escaped Cairo. "Uh oh. You said that like you've only heard bad things." He motioned toward JJ's arm. "What happened?" Even Cairo heard how genuinely concerned he sounded. He knew what it was like to have traumatic injuries.

JJ turned away and set up a shooting station. He struggled to do everything left-handed, especially hold a steady gun. "Hugh happened."

The immediate sick feeling hit like a truck. Hearing Hugh's name on the heels of a horrible flashback nearly set him back two months on his therapy. "What?" It was the only word his lips would shape. His brain had been wiped clean. Surely, he had misheard. Maybe he really was more tired than he thought.

JJ's hand shook as he tried aiming with his non-dominant arm. He growled and tossed Cairo an irritated look. "There's no way you don't know this. After all, I lost a fucking hand for you."

Something inside Cairo died a little. He felt the adult inside him shriveling, searching for the safety of being a child. "Oh. No. I didn't know."

At the sound of his voice getting smaller, JJ softened. He looked torn. "Look, I shouldn't have said that. This has just been a hard day for me, and you said your name."

"And you lost a hand for me," Cairo finished for him. "I understand. Don't worry. I'll get out of your way." No one knew better than he did what helpless rage felt like. Maybe if he was in JJ's shoes, he would shoot him. Life would have been so much more convenient for everyone if he had stayed with Hugh. No one here deserved to be tormented by Hugh just because Cairo existed.

JJ huffed. His light green eyes flashed with aggravation. "You don't have to go. This is your home. Hell, it's probably more your home than mine. I'm just some rat from the streets. Fuck, I really can't stop. What's wrong with me?"

A sad smile tugged at Cairo's lips. He understood a lot more than JJ would ever believe. "You're angry, and you're right to be." Cairo still couldn't stop sounding more like a kid than an adult, but he also couldn't let JJ think Cairo didn't deserve his rage. "Hugh bought me when I was very little. He'll never stop feeling like he owns me. Maybe he does," Cairo added absently. He shook his head, trying to shake away the darkness closing in. "You didn't deserve to get hurt because of me." Cairo swallowed. It hurt, just the same as having Hugh's hands around his neck again. "I wish I had known he hadn't given up before this happened to you. It's my fault. Don't worry. It won't happen again." He managed a sad smile and headed for the door. JJ spoke again, but Cairo didn't hear a word. His pulse pounded too loudly in his ears. Rhodes had given him six months of a beautiful life and his heart. That was more than Cairo thought he would get in this lifetime. Cairo couldn't risk Rhodes being the next person Hugh hurt. He just wished he had gotten to tell Rhodes he loved him too.

Chapter Eight

A WARM OCEAN BREEZE ruffled through Cairo's hair. He put the hood up on his old bear pajamas. He didn't dare wear anything Rhodes had bought him. Cairo kind of hated how thin they were. He had always been one to get cold easily. Cairo had always kind of resented that too. It was like that trait only highlighted how weak he was.

The secluded beach should have been such a beautiful spot. Unfortunately, the area was secluded for a reason. While no one could actually own any part of California's beaches, Hugh's property spanned miles of coastline, including a hidden port for trafficking children. This picnic table was the only thing he recalled from his earliest days with Hugh. He despised every inch of this place.

Cairo wasn't surprised he walked so easily into Hugh's territory. He supposed everyone had seen him at least once. For whatever reason, Cairo was the only boy Hugh forbade anyone else from touching. A shiver ran through Cairo. He felt sick from all the memories. Cairo supposed there had been a time when being Hugh's special little guy had been okay with him. Hell was like that, though. There were different levels. All he had known back then was he wasn't starved like the other boys. He wasn't passed around like them either. His throat swelled, and Cairo fought the growing urge to cry. He had to let the nightmares engulf him. Cairo couldn't focus on the good life he had found after his escape. He couldn't bring Rhodes here. The more minutes that passed, the deeper Cairo sank into nothingness. There was no describing the yawning hole in his chest. He'd had a lot of nightmares over the last few months where he had sat right here again, waiting on the picnic table with his feet on the bench, knowing the horrors to come.

A low, menacing chuckle sounded behind him, sounding like cannon fire to him. He started at the sound, and Cairo fucking hated that shit too. Cairo refused to turn, though. Hugh would have to come to him.

Hugh dragged his hand across the small of Cairo's back as he circled Cairo. "In my heart, I knew you'd be back. You enjoy the power you have over me too much, but you also love me."

Then Hugh was there. He physically turned Cairo sideways on the table so he could crowd Cairo's space. He toyed with Cairo's hood with shaky hands while his hungry gaze moved over Cairo's face. His sickness was on full display.

"It's good to see you out of those ridiculous big-boy clothes that pig made you wear. You're too soft for that life." Hugh lowered his voice for only Cairo's ears, making Cairo realize guards stood nearby. "I've missed you, pet. You have no idea how much I hate that I'll have to punish you for this."

An odd sense of calm settled over Cairo. Rhodes had made him strong. He wasn't scared. Still, he kept his voice as small and meek as possible. Cairo toyed with the buttons of Hugh's shirt, awkwardly unbuttoning the material one-handed until it fell open into two halves. "Do you plan to humiliate me, Daddy?" God, the question was razor blades in his throat.

A smile that sent shivers down Cairo's spine stretched across Hugh's lips. Oddly, he looked so... normal. Why hadn't Cairo ever noticed that before? Hugh could pass anyone on the street and no one would realize the pure evil they passed. That was a chilling realization.

Hugh made a small gesture and his guards left. “Since you came home willingly, I’ll grant you that one concession. Plus, you’re mine. No one else gets to see you the way I do.” Hugh slowly slid the zipper down on Cairo’s one-piece outfit. “You'd better not have grown any weird hair since I last saw you. You know how much I hate that.”

Cairo wanted to puke in his mouth, but he stayed the subservient child Hugh saw when he looked at Cairo. “Don’t be silly, Daddy. I’m a baby. Babies don’t have weird hair. We have cute hair.”

He watched Hugh get hotter and more distracted the more Cairo played his game. “Damn right. How do you plan to make up for making me sad? I can’t let this go. You need to understand you can’t do this to me again.” Hugh had worked his way between Cairo's thighs. Only a few inches remained between them.

Cairo's skin crawled. He worked up the sweetest and most innocent smile he could achieve. "Don't worry, Daddy. I won't." The sound of the gunshot was much louder than Cairo expected. A small part of him wanted to look around to see if Hugh's guards were about to attack. But Cairo couldn't look away from Hugh. He didn't know if Hugh was too shocked to react or if the bullet in his heart worked faster than he expected. Cairo wouldn't know. He had never killed anyone before. All he knew was he couldn't look away from watching the life leave Hugh's eyes. Cairo had expected—if he actually made it this far—that he would feel something. Relief. Fear. Anything. He fully expected

Hugh's guards would shoot him dead any second. Cairo felt nothing. He wasn't scared. Cairo had rid the world of a monster, and it had been much easier than he thought it would be. Even though he already knew it was an act that would save no one, since there was always another monster hiding in the shadows. He was owed this, and still. He felt nothing.

As Hugh's body dropped, it finally occurred to Cairo no one had come running. It was possible they thought Hugh had put him down and were just waiting to be instructed to clean up. Cairo still doubted he would make it, but he headed back toward the truck Rhodes had bought him. He wouldn't run. Cairo wouldn't let them chase him like the pet they saw him as, but yeah. He knew this was the end. Maybe he could be a little closer to Rhodes' gift when they mowed him down. One last small connection to the love he had found in the end. No one could steal that from him.

A rat scratched at the walls of his brain, making Rhodes want to tear off his skin. He knew they couldn't storm Hugh's home without a plan, but it was his man who had God only knew what happening to him, if he wasn't already dead. Rhodes wanted to climb the walls. He wanted to scream for everyone to get their shit together.

The Agafonov brothers wore all black and held their gear. Their LED masks were already in place as they checked to ensure they could hear and see each other. Tracker, the one who manned the high-tech van and oversaw operations, barked out orders. Rhodes knew they were moving as fast as they safely could. After all, it was their lives they put at risk for Cairo. None of that knowledge saved Rhodes' sanity.

When JJ had come to him about his encounter with Cairo, Rhodes had immediately gone in search of him. When he realized Cairo was gone, he had tracked the location of the truck he had gifted Cairo. He hadn't breathed properly since.

JJ sat in a chair against the wall of Beau's office, watching Rhodes pace. His face was pale, and Rhodes couldn't decide if he was enraged with the guy or not. He was too scared to think, and JJ could have just gone along with his day, forgetting the incident. Apparently, there had been a certain something in Cairo's manner that sent warning bells blaring inside him. It would have been easier if JJ had pretended nothing had happened. Beau was furious. Rhodes wanted to melt down.

"Oh, no. What did I miss?"

Rhodes spun so fast, he nearly fell. Cairo stood in the doorway of the office, his arms laden with a bouquet of red roses and two yellow ones. Rhodes' vision narrowed. He wondered if he would faint. Cairo had definitely taken ten years off his life. Now, here he stood, perfectly fine. He wore a T-shirt and jeans along with his work boots. He was calm. If Rhodes didn't know better, he would have thought Cairo just went to the store and back.

"What the fuck, Cairo? Are you okay?" He closed the distance between them and inspected Cairo for wounds.

"I'm fine. Are you okay?" He sounded like they had a normal conversation. Rhodes didn't know whether to laugh or shake him.

"Of course I'm not okay. You disappeared."

Cairo gave a solemn nod. He held out the red roses. "I got these for you."

Rhodes blinked, just confused as fuck. Everyone stood in shocked silence as Cairo crossed the room. He handed one of the yellow bouquets to JJ. "I'm sorry I ruined your life. No way would I have chosen that. I hope you know I would've rather stayed in that hell than let anyone get hurt in my place."

JJ blinked, still in obvious shock. He accepted the flowers.

Cairo moved to Beau's desk.

Fletch jogged into the room. He headed straight for Beau. Fletch said something close to Beau's ear no one else could hear. Beau slowly nodded before turning his attention to Cairo.

Cairo held out the last bouquet before Beau could speak. "I'm sorry for coming here and making your life harder. Thank you for letting me be friends with Kylo. I never had a friend before I came here."

Beau's face remained blank, but he accepted the flowers. After a moment, Beau cleared his throat. "Think nothing of it. I should be thanking you. It seems Hugh was found dead tonight. A single gunshot to the heart."

Every head turned Cairo's way. "That's good." Cairo sounded like he spoke about the weather.

"His guards claim it was you who killed him."

Cairo didn't react. He gave no indication that he had murdered someone tonight. "That's inconvenient. I hope that doesn't bring more grief your way."

Beau made a dismissive gesture. "It'll be a cold day in hell before I stress myself over a bunch of leaderless child predators. I'll make a call. It'll be handled." He stood. "In the meantime, I have a completely unaware husband waiting for me in bed." He tossed a glance around the room, making a sweeping round of eye contact. "He will remain unaware." Everyone nodded and mumbled their agreement about how Kylo should never know this. Beau focused on Cairo again. “You also have a man waiting for you. You scared the shit out of him. Make it right.”

Cairo nodded. “I will.”

Rhodes was shocked, on the edge of disbelief, and oddly proud as hell of the man who had stolen him.

Without looking back, Beau walked away, leaving a room full of baffled men behind.

Some muttered words of being grateful Cairo wasn’t hurt and laughingly offered to let him join the Agafonov team. All Rhodes could do was stare at Cairo as the room cleared.

Cairo chewed his bottom lip and held Rhodes’ gaze. It was obvious he was nervous but determined to not back down. Rhodes couldn't have him alone fast enough. Cairo didn't wait until the final person filed out.

"I love you." Cairo made the proclamation steady and serious. No one could doubt him.

Nothing else mattered. That realization fell over him with absolute certainty. At the end of the day, Cairo was unharmed, and he loved Rhodes.

Still, they didn't move toward each other. "I couldn't let anyone else get hurt."

Rhodes' breath left him. Cairo really had been the one to kill Hugh. He had already put two and two together, but there was something about Cairo addressing the mess head-on. His throat swelled. Rhodes wasn't dumb.

"You left here to die, didn't you? How could you do that to me?" It seemed something else mattered after all. He couldn't stop. His heart was breaking. "You stole my heart and gave me a life I never thought I could have. Did you even think about what would happen to me without you?"

Cairo blinked. His eyes filled with tears, but it was as if Cairo refused to let them fall. "You mean everything to me. But this one thing isn't about you, and I couldn't carry it any longer. When I saw what Hugh did to JJ, it was like I was back in that nightmare all over again. Except this time, I wasn't helpless, and I couldn't sleep another night knowing that monster still walked the planet." Cairo held up his hand, stopping Rhodes before he even thought to speak. "I know I could've come to you and things would've been handled. It had to be me."

Rhodes got it. It wasn't like he didn't know Cairo deserved this retribution. He just hurt for himself and the knowledge that Cairo might have died tonight while he did nothing.

Cairo slowly made the distance between them vanish, as if scared Rhodes would push him away once he got too close. Damn. Rhodes really loved him. There was no chance he would reject him in any way. Rhodes just wished Cairo understood how he felt.

Cairo slid his palms across Rhodes' sides until they met behind Rhodes' back, leaving no space between except for squished roses.

"I'm sorry I hurt you. My whole mind was consumed with hurt and anger. I thought about you, but I realize now my thoughts were all about my side of things. You're such an amazing man. All I could think was how much you've given me and how strong you've made me. I thought about how I was okay to die because I'd found you. For a moment, I held the world, and life with you was more beautiful than I could've dreamed. I thought, at least I had gotten a little love before the end. So you're right. You deserved a lot better from me than to think only about my feelings. If you're done with me, I get it. I deserve to hurt the way I made you hurt."

Truth be told, the more Cairo said, the more Rhodes wanted to turn him over his knee. But there was nothing Rhodes could say to change anything. Instead, he set his roses aside and tossed Cairo over his shoulder. Rhodes headed for the stairs, ranting the entire way.

"I love you. If you ever offer to let me go again." Rhodes tried to think of a threat, but nothing genuine came to mind. "Well, I don't know what I'll do, but you won't enjoy it." He stamped up each step. "Our relationship isn't up for leverage. You don't get to fix things by letting me go. This is real. That means we always stay and fight." Inside their bedroom, he kicked the door behind him and tossed Cairo on the bed. Rhodes held Cairo's stare. "I'm yours."

"Okay." Cairo looked innocent and accepting. From his spot on the bed, Cairo looked way too inviting. Cairo's tongue shot out and brushed along his bottom lip, as if suddenly nervous again. "Since you're mine, does that mean I can touch you?"

Rhodes fought a smile. "Any damn time you want." He had no idea why he still sounded angry.

Cairo shifted onto his knees. "I have my shoes on the bed. That seems like something you should scold me about." Cairo gave him puppy-dog eyes. "Maybe even spank me."

A smile exploded across Rhodes' face. Rhodes had always known Cairo was the one in control. That was fine. "I don't know if that's exactly spanking territory, especially since I threw you on the bed. But you should take your boots off, just the same." While holding Cairo's stare, Rhodes peeled his shirt up and over his head. Cairo caught on quick. He was out of his shoes in no time.

Rhodes' hands moved to his belt.

Cairo watched him pull the leather piece loose. His gaze moved from Rhodes unbuttoning his jeans to holding Rhodes' stare again. "Is it okay if I still call you Daddy, even though I'm not little anymore?"

Rhodes stopped unzipping his jeans. This was an important conversation. "I am still your daddy." He moved closer until he had Cairo toppled on the bed again, and he covered Cairo like a blanket. "Your sugar daddy." Rhodes infused some humor into his voice, hoping he didn't insult Cairo.

Cairo nodded. He looked like this was the most serious conversation he had ever had. "That's true. You are very sugary."

Rhodes snorted. He couldn't help it. Being with Cairo was so much fun.

Cairo shoved his hands down the back of Rhodes' loose jeans. "That makes me want to lick you, but too much has happened today. I need you inside me so you can stop the shaking in my bones."

It hit Rhodes. Cairo was nowhere near as calm as he appeared. Cairo had simply mastered the art of hiding fear. He had himself tightly contained, but if Rhodes didn't give him an outlet soon, all those emotions would flood out and break him down.

"I've got you."

Rhodes didn't hesitate to do whatever it took to get Cairo out of his clothes. In no time, they were nude, and Rhodes' lube-coated fingers worked at stretching Cairo. Cairo never looked away from him. It was like Rhodes was the only thing holding him together. Rhodes couldn't take it. He shifted positions and impaled Cairo.

Cairo's chin tilted upward, and the sexiest of moans left his perfect lips. Rhodes couldn't resist his exposed neck. He dipped his head and sucked on the spot directly below Cairo's Adam's apple. With one hand holding Cairo at the angle Rhodes wanted him in, Rhodes pumped his hips. He kept a steady but slow rhythm. Not only did Rhodes want Cairo to feel his love, but he needed the connection too. Cairo wasn't the only one still shaking inside even though everything turned out okay. The alternative still danced on his brain and scared the shit out of Rhodes.

Cairo's fingers dug into Rhodes' back as he strained to take what he wanted. "Please? I need you."

Rhodes couldn't deny Cairo anything. He hadn't been exaggerating; Cairo fully owned him. He chose another spot to suck as he picked up the pace. Rhodes followed the sounds Cairo made. It got harder for him to hold out. His mind was locked in pleasure mode. Rhodes couldn't think about anything but the way Cairo's body made him feel.

Rhodes buried his face against Cairo's chest and made noises he couldn't control. When cum hit him in the chin,

Rhodes lost his mind. He used Cairo's body, taking him exactly the way Rhodes needed.

"Goddamn, Cairo. You can't ever leave me. I've never been as close to insanity as I was tonight. You're every fucking thing to me. I don't exist without you." The closer he got to explosion, the less sense his words made. He was right there.

"I want to spend the rest of my life with you." Cairo's whispered words pushed Rhodes over the cliff. He cried Cairo's name as an orgasm pulsed through him, rendering him blind and deaf. All Rhodes knew was ecstasy and pure love. His mouth covered Cairo's as the last waves passed. He still couldn't get enough. Rhodes had to hang on to their connection any way he could.

As his skin cooled, the entire day washed over Rhodes again, all the way to the second Cairo said he wanted to spend the rest of his life with Rhodes. Cairo would absolutely get his wish. Rhodes planned never to let Cairo leave his sight again.

Chapter Nine

From Rhodes' lap, Cairo inspected the club that had once come to his rescue with new eyes. He hadn't been back to The PlayPen since the night he left with Rhodes. Now he realized how many people there were like him. About three-quarters of the Littles were just that. However, there was a whole other quarter that were somewhere between Littles and adults. Not quite grownups but also not in the pajama stage anymore. Cairo wished he had noticed that sooner.

He glanced down at himself. While Kylo had done his makeup, making him look pretty, Cairo wore board shorts and a tank top. But his favorite part of the outfit was his hot pink sneakers. He loved bright colors. Somewhere along the way, Cairo realized he wasn't a baby anymore, but neither did he care to be an adult. He couldn't handle the full responsibility of being a grown-up. While his entire mind recoiled at the idea of Little sexual play now, he still desperately needed Rhodes to be his daddy. Thankfully, he seemed to be exactly what Rhodes needed too. They fit. Rhodes craved someone who belonged to him and him alone. He was a caretaker, and Cairo's mental health stability depended on someone else being in control. Rhodes was in charge. He spoiled Cairo and did everything for him. Meanwhile, Cairo got to be Rhodes' soft spot, his peace, and his best friend. They got to love each other with a fierceness neither of them had before each other. He thought they were beautiful.

Cairo snuggled deeper into Rhodes' hold and went back to eyeing his surroundings. Beau sat at a card table, holding Kylo while playing poker with his sons, and some other men. Fletch sat on the floor with his back against the wall. He had his legs stretched out in front of him with his feet crossed at the ankles. For some reason, he had his arms crossed and looked angry. Rhodes and he sat next to him. JJ sat across from them on the other side of Fletch's legs. They had their own little circle going on. JJ seemed miserable.

Looking at him, it dawned on Cairo how young JJ was. It hurt his chest knowing he was the reason JJ's life had been altered forever. Nonetheless, JJ seemed determined to forgive him. Cairo couldn't believe JJ had accepted their invitation to go out with them tonight. Unfortunately, Cairo had a bad feeling their choice of locations highlighted something unhappy about his life.

Cairo might have watched him all night, trying to puzzle him out, if Rhodes hadn't kissed his ear.

"I have something for you."

Cairo immediately perked up. "Really?"

Rhodes didn't answer. He slid his hand down Cairo's left arm until he reached his hand. While Cairo watched, Rhodes slipped a ring onto Cairo's ring finger.

It was beautiful. The piece looked like a panda's head, except the design was made of diamonds. He had never seen anything like it. Cairo fell in love immediately.

"Oh my gosh. It's beautiful." He brought the ring close to his face and inspected the piece. "Is this my engagement ring?"

Rhodes kissed his neck. "Yeah. Is it okay?"

Was it okay? Rhodes never stopped blowing him away. All it had taken was for Cairo to say he wanted to spend the rest of his life with Rhodes, and Rhodes immediately bought Cairo a ring. There had been no question that they would get married. They were a set.

"It's perfect." Cairo whispered the words, only for them to be drowned out by a Little throwing a full-blown temper tantrum nearby. He literally kept moving to different spots near their circle and throwing himself on the floor. The guy kicked and screamed while everyone ignored him. Unfortunately, the guy was ruining Cairo's moment. He couldn't have that, and Rhodes deserved better.

"Hold on, okay?"

Rhodes didn't argue when Cairo stood, but he looked confused. Cairo didn't stop to explain before heading toward a stack of baby blankets. They smelled freshly laundered, and Cairo fought the urge to bury his face in the pile. Instead, he grabbed the one on top. He stormed his way to tantrum baby and kneeled at his side. Cairo tossed the blanket over him, buying him a second of peace due to shocking the guy.

Cairo leaned in close and practically hissed at him. "Take a nap, baby. Either that or go eat something. You're ruining my big night. If I have to come over here again, I'm bringing a water gun. You're too big to be showing out."

Cairo stood, intent on going straight back to Rhodes' lap. Before he took a step, he noticed a pair of boys sitting close by who seemed out of place for some reason. They were too stoic—like they didn't feel comfortable or welcome. He couldn't explain it, but that was a sentiment he understood.

Cairo waved for them to come with him. "Come play with us."

The pair stood, both clutching books to their chests. They didn't speak, but they followed Cairo to their little group.

Cairo reclaimed his seat on Rhodes' lap. "Look who I found." He chirped the words happily as if he had always known the pair. One who looked especially shy sat between Cairo and Fletch. The other plopped down on JJ's lap. While JJ looked shocked, he didn't push the guy away.

Cairo made the rounds, pointing out everyone. "That's Fletch, JJ." He motioned over his shoulder. "Rhodes, and I'm Cairo."

Shy guy glanced up quickly. "July." He immediately withdrew again.

"Awww. That's cute."

A blush tinted July's cheeks.

Cairo focused on the guy on JJ's lap.

He bounced a little, obviously excited at the idea of having new friends. “I’m Bean.”

That one woke up JJ. “Bean?” He sounded almost incredulous.

Bean nodded. “That’s what everyone calls me here. You know, for Jelly Bean.” He twisted to look at JJ and spread his arms for a second. “I’m round, like a bean.”

Fletch was not having it. “What the fuck? You’re not round.”

Bean shrugged. “It’s okay. Round is my favorite shape. It could be worse.”

JJ’s brow was furrowed so deep, he looked ready to fight someone. “I’m not calling you that. What’s your real name?”

For the first time, Bean looked nervous. He fiddled with his book while his deep green gaze shot in every direction. Between his dinosaur two-piece pajamas and big eyes, he looked innocent as hell.

JJ didn't give up. "Whisper it to me. I won't tell."

Bean's shoulders visibly relaxed. A sweet smile touched his lips. He leaned close and whispered against JJ's ear.

JJ smiled. He looked even younger than Cairo had thought earlier. "I love that." He tugged Bean into a more comfortable-looking position on his lap—like settling in. "If you turn the pages, I'll read to you."

Bean looked happy. He seemed completely oblivious or unconcerned about JJ's missing hand. Cairo desperately wanted that happiness for JJ. He needed someone.

While JJ read, July stared at the carpet and didn't even look at his book.

Fletch snagged July's waist and towed him between his legs. He urged July to lean back against his chest while he opened the book. "Let's see what this is all about."

July nodded, but his expression gave nothing away. His hazel eyes and smattering of freckles made him adorable as could be, but—like Cairo—he wasn't dressed like a Little. He was more like Kylo, wildly put together like he had stopped halfway through playing in the dress-up area and just plopped down with a book. He wore a regular t-shirt with an elaborate princess skirt over his jeans. July was missing a shoe and wore a single lace glove. A tiara hung by a miracle and a prayer off the side of his head.

Fletch gently untangled the piece before setting it aside. "We'll put this here so I can see the book."

July nodded and calmly relaxed into Fletch's hold.

Rhodes' lips skimmed his ear. "I guess you're feeling pretty proud of yourself right now. Look at you, matchmaking."

That hadn't been Cairo's plan, but he was happy to have found new friends. He opened his mouth to respond, and tantrum guy screeched at the top of his lungs, like just coming back from a bathroom break and getting back to work.

Cairo sighed. "I'll be back. I need to find a water gun." Even to his ears, he sounded done. Being a big boy could be exhausting. He didn't have the patience for babies, but something about this one really pissed him off. It was like he targeted their group with his antics. But he didn't know Cairo, and he was about to find out. Cairo wanted to savor the wonderful moment of knowing Rhodes would be his forever. So this dude would shut the fuck up if Cairo had to tie him to a chair and gag him. That was a promise.

It had honestly been a fun night watching Cairo torment Fletch's ex, Sammie. But he equally hated the brat for ruining his night with Cairo. Rhodes was more than a little grateful to be on the way home. Darkness engulfed them along with the quiet. It didn't even matter they were crammed in a huge SUV with Beau, Kylo, Fletch, and JJ. Rhodes was technically working. As long as Beau was near, Rhodes was on guard. He would never let anything happen to the man who had given him the means to take care of Cairo the way he deserved.

Kylo noticed Cairo petting his ring. He sat forward and focused on Cairo. "Is that an engagement ring? Oh my God."

Cairo chuckled and bounced a little, making Rhodes smile. "Yes! Look. It's so cute."

Kylo inspected the ring. "It's adorable. When are you getting married?"

Cairo looked to Rhodes, the way he did for nearly every decision. Life felt too hard for Cairo. His trauma made even the small things too heavy to carry.

Rhodes answered on their behalf. "As soon as possible. Probably my next day off."

Kylo looked at Beau.

Beau released a small sigh—like indulging Kylo wasn't all he lived for. Despite the sound, a small smile hovered on his lips, and he pulled his phone from his shirt pocket. "I'll make the calls."

Kylo's smile grew. He happy-clapped. "Yay! Your makeup is already pretty, and you can borrow anything you want from me. This'll be so much fun."

Cairo looked every bit as confused as Rhodes. "What?"

Kylo made a dismissive gesture. "Your wedding, silly. Beau will have the whole thing set up before we even get home. Then we're heading to Hawaii next week for three months. You can treat the trip like a honeymoon."

Rhodes bit back a huff. He hadn't told Cairo about Hawaii yet for just that reason. The Bosi family had a second home there. Rhodes had hoped to marry Cairo the day after tomorrow and then go straight to Hawaii as a surprise.

Cairo looked his way.

Rhodes flashed him a smile, expecting any reaction.

Then Cairo's eyes filled with tears, and Rhodes had definitely not been prepared for that. "We're about to get married." The awe in Cairo's voice eased the grip his tears had taken on Rhodes' heart.

"We are."

Cairo sniffed and wiped his eyes before launching himself toward Rhodes. He kissed Rhodes all over his face while Rhodes laughed.

"Congrats, man."

"Yeah, congrats."

Fletch and JJ showed their support while Cairo let out his excitement. Rhodes knew Beau well enough to know there would be a full wedding before the end of the night.

Cairo settled down but had somehow ended up on Rhodes' lap. He lowered his voice, keeping his words for Rhodes, even though there was no doubt everyone else heard. "I love you, Daddy."

Rhodes kissed Cairo's forehead. "I love you too, baby." He pressed his lips against Cairo's ear. "You'll see. I'll be the best husband."

Cairo snuggled close. "I know." He stroked Rhodes' collarbone, petting him. "We'll have the best life."

Rhodes' throat swelled as Cairo fell into a happy chatter, talking about everything under the sun while painting a beautiful picture of their future. There had been a time when Rhodes had lived on the street and never imagined his life turning out this way. Then he met this flawless man who gave him purpose, and now he couldn't picture any type of life that didn't include Cairo. He was the luckiest daddy alive. Cairo would always know it.

Keep your eye out for the next The PlayPen,

About the Author

Charity Parkerson is an award-winning and multi-published author with several companies. Born with no filter from her brain to her mouth, she decided to take this odd quirk and insert it in her characters. One of her greatest loves is writing morally gray characters. You'll find them scattered throughout her hundreds of titles.

*Nine-time Readers' Favorite Award Winner

*2015 Passionate Plume Award Finalist

*2013 Reviewers' Choice Award Winner

*2012 ARRA Finalist for Favorite Paranormal Romance

*Five-time winner of The Mistress of the Darkpath

Connect with her online:

*Sign up for her newsletter: https://bit.ly/charityparkersonnewsletter

*Join her readers' group on Facebook: http://bit.ly/CharitysTribe

*Website: https://www.charityparkerson.com

*A list of her social media accounts and giveaways all in one place: http://hy.page/charityparkerson

www.ingramcontent.com/pod-product-compliance
Lightning Source LLC
LaVergne TN
LVHW010656110826
845149LV00014B/3117